WALT DISNEP PICTURES presents

Shipwrecked

WALT DISNEY PICTURES presents

Shipwrecked

A Novel by B.B. Hiller

Based on the Motion Picture from
Walt Disney Pictures
Executive Producer Nigel Wooll
Produced by John M. Jacobsen
Based on the Screenplay by Nils Gaup &
Bob Foss & Greg Dinner and Nick Thiel
Directed by Nils Gaup

SCHOLASTIC INC.
New York Toronto London Auckland Sydney

ISBN 0-590-44775-0

12 11 10 9 8 7 6 5 4 3 2 1   1 2 3 4 5 6/9

Printed in the U.S.A.   01

First Scholastic printing, March 1991

Walt Disney PICTURES presents

Shipwrecked

Prologue

Three men huddled silently at a table in the rear, unaware of the roar and bustle of the rowdy crowd at The Buccaneer Pub in London. From time to time, they looked across the room to a man standing at the bar. He wore the uniform of the Royal British Navy.

At the table, one of the men, the leader, spoke softly to the others. A shock of black hair dropped over the man's face, calling attention to his angular features — a long, thin nose, jutted jawline, and a pointy chin. The two most remarkable things about his face though, were his piercing gray eyes and a long scar that ran across his right cheek. It was a memento from the last time anybody's sword had been faster than his. That had been a long time ago.

The two with him were sailors, his mates. On the surface they were no different from the hundreds of others who crowded the room at the pub. Like the others, they'd traveled the world and gotten into their share of mischief. The difference was that they sailed under the flag of no nation but their own. Their flag was the Jolly Roger. They were pirates.

The scar-faced leader nodded a signal. The two sailors rose unnoticed and left the pub. When they were gone, the leader rose. He pulled up the collar of his great coat to mask his trademark scar, stood up, and slowly made his way to the bar, brushing past the British naval officer.

The officer looked up, irritated. Then looked again. There was something familiar about the man whose collar hid his face.

Pretending drunkenness, the scar-faced man ordered a mug of ale. When it arrived, he picked up the mug clumsily and put it to his lips. He managed to pour most of the frothy contents on himself, some on the bar, and some on the British officer.

"Aarrrrgh!" he roared, lowering his collar to wipe his face with his sleeve. Then, still apparently angry at the spilled ale, he swung around and marched out the door of the pub.

The hair, the angular face, the gray eyes, the rude manner. They all struck a faint chord of familiarity in the British officer's memory. But when he saw the scar, he knew.

"Merrick," he said, muttering the name to himself. The name belonged to the cruelest, most notorious pirate of the seven seas.

"Merrick!" he said it again louder and then ran in pursuit.

By the time the officer made his way through the crowd and onto the street, Merrick was out of sight. The officer, a man named Howell, followed the sound of Merrick's footsteps retreating in the dark.

Merrick led him through the twisted streets and back alleys of London's harbor area. Howell pressed on, determined to catch the scoundrel who raided ships and murdered their crews. He followed the man he had sworn in his oath of office to wipe from the seas.

And then he had Merrick trapped. The man had unwittingly turned down a narrow blind alley with a wall at the end of it. There was no way out. The two stood and faced one another.

"It *is* you, Merrick — in London!"

The gray eyes flashed in the dim light. "And it's you, Officer Howell — in a predicament!"

The two men who had preceded Merrick out of the pub emerged from the shadows, behind Howell. All three pirates drew their pistols. It was Howell who was trapped!

"Have you taken your piracy to the streets?" Howell asked.

"Wherever it pays," Merrick said simply. "I hear you've been commissioned to a merchant ship bound for Australia and Calcutta, and I'll thank you to give me your sailing orders."

Howell didn't move. Merrick's men tore open Howell's coat, reached into his pocket, and found the pack of documents they wanted. Merrick himself took Howell's hat and put it on his head.

"What do you think, mates? Am I royal enough?"

Suddenly Howell realized what the pirates were up to. "You'll never get away with impersonating me!"

"Wouldn't you like to be there to see it?" Merrick put his arm around Howell's shoulders. "A pirate captain welcomed aboard a merchant ship." He paused to enjoy Howell's reaction. "But there can only be one of you, and it's going to be me!"

Merrick released Howell, turning him over to his mates whose instructions were clear and whose pistols were ready to do the job.

Chapter 1

Haakon was afraid. It was a familiar feeling. He was often afraid. This time he was afraid of the boys who were chasing him across the fields and hills of his homeland in Norway. He paused to get his breath, barely noticing the snow-covered hillsides leading down to the fjord and the ocean beyond. All he saw was that the boys were catching up to him. He picked up his bucket and began running again.

He stumbled on a rock, righted himself, and continued his flight. He slipped on some ice and banged his knee. It didn't matter. He had to escape the bullies who were after him. He stood up and ran.

Haakon was small for his fourteen years, but he was clever. This time, however, he wasn't clever enough, for he'd forgotten that the trail he'd chosen ran right into the bank of a wide stream. Even though it was April, the stream was still half frozen and dangerous. Haakon halted fearfully.

"What's the matter, Haakon? It's just a little stream. How about a swim?" Ole taunted him.

The other boys laughed at the fear that showed so plainly on Haakon's pale face. One stood behind Haakon and nudged him toward the edge.

Haakon stared at the black water whirling beneath the spots of ice. "No! No! Please!"

Finally, still laughing at Haakon's babyish fright, they released him, allowing him to drop safely into the snow. He sidled away from the frozen riverbank like a crab and, when he was far enough away to feel safe, he fought back the only way he knew.

"You wait until my father comes home!" he said. "He'll take care of you — all of you!" He glared at Ole, the ringleader.

"Your father isn't coming home," Ole said cruelly. "He's lost at sea!"

"He is not! He'll be home soon!" Haakon retorted, but the hard part, the thing he was most afraid of, was that Ole could be right.

"Well, he owes my father so much money, he'd be better off lost!" Ole said, and laughed again.

Haakon knew that might be true, too. Ole's father, Wernes, owned the general store in town. As long as Haakon's father was at sea, the family had little cash to pay what they owed. Unless his father returned soon with a purse filled with his seafaring pay . . . Haakon was too afraid to think about that.

As a final, parting insult, Ole picked up Haakon's bucket and set it on a fast-moving chunk of ice in the stream. Then he hopped across the stream himself, jumping from rock to rock, and disappeared with his fellow bullies in tow.

For Haakon, it was a day like any other.

It took him forty-five minutes, chasing the stream downhill, to coax the ice chunk with the bucket to a place where he could finally nab the thing and continue on his way home. His mother would be worried about him, but the Haakonsen family couldn't afford a new bucket.

A sleigh pulled up in front of the family farm just as Haakon arrived with his battered bucket. Two men lowered themselves from the seat. His sisters hugged one of the men. Haakon couldn't believe his eyes.

"Papa?"

This was Haakon's dream come true!

His father reached out his arms. Haakon ran to them.

"Papa, Papa, I thought you might never come home!" he cried.

Mr. Haakonsen held his son tight. "I promised you I would, didn't I?"

Then Haakon noticed two things at the same time. His father held a cane, and with the first step he took, Haakon knew he had come home because he was hurt. The second thing he noticed was the man who had come with his father.

"I wouldn't have made it home if it weren't for Jens here," Mr. Haakonsen said, answering his son's unasked questions. "My leg got tangled in a jib line and I was knocked over the side of the ship. Jens jumped in and cut me free before I drowned."

Haakon tried to envision the scene as it must have

happened. What he saw were the acts of two men with more courage than he could imagine. Haakon gulped with fear.

"Don't listen to your dad's tall tales," Jens said, clapping Haakon on the back. "I didn't jump in to save him. I was just needing a bath!"

Everybody laughed, even Haakon. The laughter masked his shivering fear.

It was wonderful to have Papa home. The dinner table seemed to glow with warmth and happiness. Haakon, his mother, and his sisters, Rakel and Sarah, listened with rapt attention as Papa and Jens told them stories from their voyage. They laughed and hugged. Haakon was sure having Papa home meant that everything would be different now.

When dinner was finished, Mrs. Haakonsen and Haakon's sisters cleared the table. Haakon remained seated with the men. It made him feel adult for the first time in his life.

"Isn't it time you showed Haakon what you brought for him?" Jens asked.

"Something for me, Papa?"

His father smiled and nodded. Slowly, ceremoniously, he reached into his coat pocket. He pulled out a scroll of paper, bound with a red ribbon.

"It's something I always dreamed about when I was your age," Mr. Haakonsen said.

Haakon felt the excitement in the air. He nearly burst with curiosity. Then his father handed the scroll to him.

Haakon unrolled it. There was a jumble of letters

and words in a language he barely knew. It looked like English. The only thing he recognized was his own name.

"It's a commission, Haakon, on my ship, the *Flora*. You're to be the new ship's boy."

Haakon felt a wave of fear. No. It couldn't be. The water, the ship, the dangers . . . he cast his eyes to the floor. It was one thing if Ole knew he was afraid, but he couldn't let his father see his fear. His eyes lit on his father's crutch.

"Nils, he's so young," Mama said.

Papa leaned forward, putting his hand on Haakon's arm. "You're ready, aren't you, son?"

Haakon stuttered. "Papa, I-I-I — "

"Sure, Haakon's ready," Jens broke in. "He's as ready to be a sailor as I was at his age. But he couldn't possibly go now."

"I couldn't?" Haakon said, the relief apparent to everybody.

"How do you think your father could work this farm with that leg of his? No, Haakon will have to stay here for the spring planting."

Papa looked at Haakon, then at Jens, then at Mama, Rakel, and Sarah. Finally, he spoke. "Jens is right. I can't afford to let you go. Not now. You're needed too much here. I'm sorry, Haakon," Papa said.

Haakon hoped his father hadn't seen his fear. Nor did he want him to see his relief.

"I can wait, Papa," he said.

Chapter 2

The signs of trouble were soon all around. When the Haakonsens went to Wernes' General Store, Wernes told Papa that he would have to pay his bill soon. Ole gloated, all the while licking on a sweet peppermint stick — a luxury Haakon's family could not afford.

Papa told Wernes that he could not pay the bill, yet. Wernes told Papa that he would not foreclose on the Haakonsen farm, yet.

At night, as Haakon lay in bed, he overheard his parents talking in the next room. The crops hadn't even been planted and already all they would earn from this year's crops was promised to others, mostly Wernes. Papa tried to borrow money from the bank in town and from once-wealthy friends, but times were bad. Nobody had anything to lend.

"I dreamed of coming home from sea a rich man," Papa told Mama. "Instead, I've come back a cripple who can't keep this little farm. If only Haakon were older, if only he wanted to go to sea — "

Haakon felt the familiar fear. He pulled the covers over his head.

For a while, life went on almost normally. The family waited for spring, when they could plant their crops. They waited for the hope that spring always brings, the promise of new life and renewal.

That spring, however, it never came. What came instead was Wernes and the sheriff. What made it all the worse for Haakon was that Ole came, too, ready to deliver the ultimate taunt.

"This is our farm now," Ole said to Haakon. "You have to get off. *Tomorrow!*" There was no mistaking the gloat in his voice.

"But this is our home," Mama protested. She looked to the sheriff for help.

He shook his head. "I hate this part of the job, Maggie, but you can't pay your debt."

There was a silence in the room. Haakon wanted to hide, but he knew that now, for once, he could not run, he could not hide, he could not even pull the covers over his head. The truth was there, plain as day.

He swallowed hard and spoke. "I'm paying the debt."

Everyone turned to him. "I'm going to sea," he explained. Ole gaped. That gave Haakon the confidence he needed. He crossed the room and handed his papers to Wernes to show him. "I'm going to be ship's boy on the *Flora*," he said finally.

"Are you sure, Haakon?" his father asked.

He smiled and nodded, trying to show a confidence he did not feel. But he also did not feel the same fear that had been gnawing at him. He'd made up his mind, and that was good.

"Haakon's going to be a sailor?" Ole asked. Then, before anybody could answer, he began laughing. Wernes squeezed his arm to stop the laughter, but Ole had still managed to hurt Haakon.

Wernes turned to Papa. "They don't pay a ship's boy what they pay an experienced sailor," he said.

"He'll receive half of my wages."

"So he'd have to work *two* years to pay the debt. Are you agreeing to that?"

"Ask my son if he agrees," Papa said.

Once again, everyone looked at Haakon. Once again, he spoke. "I agree," he said.

Wernes shrugged then and turned to Papa. "Deal," he said. He gave Haakon a pen and told him to sign some papers. Haakon took the pen and signed his name as his mother had showed him, scratching the letters carefully on the paper.

"Good luck, boy," the sheriff said, patting him on the shoulder. Haakon was glad for the encouragement. He thought he would need all the luck he could get.

Then, as quickly as they'd arrived, Ole, Wernes, and the sheriff were gone. Haakon was alone with his parents and his sisters and his decision. Suddenly he realized what his decision would mean. He felt terribly self-conscious. Looking for something to cover his discomfort, he picked up a chunk of bread from the dinner table and bit into it.

"Maggie," Papa said to Mama. "Would you be fixing Haakon and me a cup of coffee? It's time a man who's going to sea had his first cup."

Mama busied herself at the stove. Papa sat down next to Haakon.

Chapter 3

Haakon trailed Jens through the maze of bales, crates, and cartons that led to the gangplank that led to the *Flora*, that led to — he didn't know what.

He could still hear the warm farewells from his family, feel the hugs from his mother and his sisters, see the good-luck waves from his friends as he and Jens had driven the sled away from the family farm and down to the sea.

"Look after him, Jens," Papa had said.

"Like he was my own," Jens pledged. Then he'd started up the team of horses and driven away before Haakon's family could see the tears.

The ship's three masts rose from the decks above her massive hull where the cargo was being stored for the long journey ahead. Haakon felt the fear he knew so well. He wished for the comfort and familiarity of home. Automatically, his hand went to his pocket. He drew out the pearl-handled knife his father had given him.

"This was given to me by my first captain," Papa

had said. "He said it would always bring me home safe — and it always has."

Haakon tucked it back into his pocket. Just knowing it was there made him feel better.

An hour later Haakon found himself standing in front of Captain Madsen, his employer. The captain looked at him expectantly.

"Haakon Haakonsen, the new ship's boy," Haakon said, saluting awkwardly.

"Ah, Nils' boy," he said, examining Haakon from where he sat behind his desk. "Tell me, your father's a big man. Why are you so puny?"

"I don't know, sir," Haakon replied.

"Well, Mr. Haakonsen, I have this to say to you: There's no room aboard this ship for children. You'll work hard, and you'll be a sailor, or I'll put you off in London!"

"Oh, no, sir! You can't. I have to work for two years — "

"My word on this ship is law, Mister," Captain Madsen cut him off. "Don't ever question that."

"Yes, sir," Haakon said, saluting again, hoping it might erase his blunder.

"Now, how's your father's leg?"

"Getting better, sir." Haakon's right hand remained glued to his eyebrow.

"Good. Go find the bosun. He'll put you to work. You're dismissed."

Haakon didn't move.

"That means *leave*, boy!"

He fled.

* * *

Haakon could hardly believe all the activity on deck when he got there. The final cargo was stowed, the sails were readied for the journey. Everywhere he looked there was activity, and Haakon had no idea what any of it was. He particularly didn't know where the bosun was.

He found Jens, high above him. The sailor was climbing around the rigging of the main mast, tightening knots, adding line, checking winches. He moved about effortlessly thirty feet above the deck. When he'd secured the final section of rigging he signaled, and two mates winched a plank up to him. He stretched out on it lazily, lounging with his hat tilted over his eyes while the dangerous mechanism lowered him to the deck.

Haakon's jaw dropped in awe.

"Nothing to it, kid, once you get the hang of it," Jens said easily. Haakon wondered if there would ever be a day when he could do something like that, but he knew there was a big difference between him and Jens. Jens wasn't afraid of anything.

"I'll never learn how to do that," Haakon said.

"I'll teach you right now."

"I'm supposed to see the bosun," Haakon said.

Jens pointed him out, and Haakon introduced himself.

"Come for your orders, have you?"

"Yes, sir," Haakon said. He knew better than to salute.

"I've got just the job for you. Did you see Jens tying a knot to that piece of rigging on the foremast?"

"Oh, yes, sir," Haakon said.

"Go untie it at once."

"Untie it, sir?"

"You heard me!"

Two mates, Steine and Berg, offered to help. Haakon didn't know what help anybody could be. The knot the bosun had pointed to was up at the top of the mast, more than thirty feet above the deck. Haakon, afraid to climb to the loft of his family barn, afraid to stand by the bank of a stream of water, was somehow going to have to get up to the top of the mast. Help wouldn't be enough.

"Can't leave those little buggers tied longer than a few minutes," Berg said. "Or they, uh, they — "

"They snap the foremast right in half!" Steine explained.

The bosun pulled the plank over for Haakon to sit on. "Come on, we'll hoist you up," he said, offering the seat to Haakon.

Haakon was too scared to protest.

"Wait, you almost forgot the blindfold!" Steine cried out. "We wouldn't want the boy to get dizzy and fall to his death." He pulled the scarf off his neck and began tying it around Haakon's head.

"But Jens wasn't blindfolded," Haakon said, confused.

"He had his eyes closed," the bosun said. "Don't need a blindfold when you're as experienced a seaman as Jens."

"Here we go!" Berg said, and Haakon flew into the air.

He could feel himself rising. Up, up, up he went.

Even without seeing, he knew he was ten, twenty, and then thirty feet up. He clutched the plank with one hand and reached for the knot above him with the other. His hand struck wood. He'd reached the crossbeam at the top of the mast.

Haakon felt fear as he had never known it before. One wrong move and he'd tumble helplessly to the deck or, even worse, to the water.

Thoughts of home flooded him. He remembered why he was there. He had to do his best. The captain had to let him stay on the ship. His whole family was relying on him.

He reached above the crossbeam, feeling for the knot he was to untie. There was only air. He would have to stand up on the narrow plank. He shifted his weight, put one foot on the plank and stood up. The boat heaved to the right, swinging the plank precariously.

"Whoa! Hey! Help!" Haakon shouted.

And then, suddenly, Haakon heard laughter. It wasn't laughter thirty feet beneath him, it was laughter right next to him.

He yanked off the blindfold and discovered to his surprise that he was dangling a mere three feet above the deck!

The look on his face made the bosun, Berg, and Steine laugh even harder and they were soon joined by all of the ship's mates. Even Jens was smiling at the absurd sight.

"Welcome to the *Flora*, young Haakon," the bosun said, when he could talk through the snorts of laughter. "Everyone has to be initiated!"

Jens offered Haakon a hand to help him down from the plank.

"Aye, bosun," Jens said. "And I remember well your initiation. The only difference between this and that was that we had to clean up the deck when you were done!"

The crew then had a laugh at the bosun's expense.

Jens led Haakon away to show him the rest of the ship. In good time, Jens demonstrated a safe way for a sailor to climb the ship's rigging. Haakon followed him, doing everything he said, all the while trying to keep from looking down. Finally they sat, side by side in a net formed by the rigging at the top of the mast.

Haakon dared to look down. Although it was a long way and a fall would surely be fatal, Haakon felt secure with Jens there to show him all the steps. He also learned that being thirty feet above the deck was nowhere near as bad as dreading it had been.

Jens demonstrated how to tie a knot and then handed the rope to Haakon to try. "A lot of men, older than you, have panicked, lost control, during an 'initiation.' You were brave, Haakon." Haakon hardly believed the words as he heard them. "My first voyage was on a Spanish trader, and my initiation was to inspect the anchor chain while we were in *tiburón*-infested water. That's Spanish for shark. If you ever want to see me jump to the masthead in a shot, just shout *'Tiburón!'* "

Jens examined the knot Haakon tied for him and

nodded, satisfied. "See, being up here is kind of fun."

Haakon swallowed hard. He was there and at least he wasn't terrified, but it wasn't his idea of fun. As usual, Jens understood what he was thinking. "Look," Jens continued, "do your work and don't ask for help. Otherwise the other men won't respect you. That could end up costing you your life."

Haakon heard those words, every one of them.

As the rigging trick had been Haakon's initiation to the crew of the *Flora*, the next few weeks were his initiation to the life of a sailor. The *Flora* was bound for London, its last port of call before the open sea. They would be taking on the remainder of their cargo and a few seamen. Each day until they reached London, Haakon knew he had to learn, to do, to work. Even the bosun's jokes couldn't distract him. Although he was afraid of the heights, the water, and the jests from the bosun and the mates, he was even more afraid of Captain Madsen, who could put him ashore in England, condemning the Haakonsen farm forever.

He cleaned the decks, tied knots, hauled garbage, hoisted sails, climbed ladders, studied the compass, held the wheel. Every day he followed orders, did his work, and learned. And then came the words he'd been waiting for, and dreading.

"Land ahoy!"

Soon after that, he found himself back in the

captain's cabin, awaiting the decision whether he would go or stay.

"It's a long journey and very hard passage," Captain Madsen began. "I don't take the lives of my crew lightly. Every man must be fit or no one is safe. Do you understand?"

Haakon understood all too well. The captain couldn't take a chance on a kid who didn't know the difference between the mainsail and the foresail. Lives depended on experience.

"I've been trying very hard, sir," Haakon said, defending himself.

"Let me show you something," Captain Madsen said, removing something from a drawer. "Have you ever seen one of these?"

Haakon took it from the captain. It was a small frame. He opened it up.

"It's called a photograph. Look at it."

It was like a painting, but different. Almost as if the moment had been captured, in shades of gray.

Haakon was sure the captain was just trying to break the bad news gently.

"Captain, please don't put me off in London. My family's depending on me!"

"Look at the photograph, my boy."

Haakon looked. Two men stood side by side. One was — it was his father! The other was Captain Madsen.

"Your father and I had this taken in London. I want you to have it. It'll remind you of home during the long voyage."

The full meaning sunk in. Haakon couldn't hold back his grin. He saluted.

"Aye aye, sir!" he said. "I mean, thank you."

"Don't thank me too soon," Captain Madsen said. "After this voyage, you may wish I'd sent you home."

"I don't think so, sir," Haakon said, knowing that only after the voyage would he have a home to return to.

Chapter 4

London was unlike anything Haakon could have imagined. There were more people crowding the docks than lived in his whole town.

The streets were filled with merchants selling their wares and urchins stealing them. An organ-grinder made sweet music while a monkey collected coins for him. Haakon had none to give him. Policemen hauled thieves off to Old Bailey to stand trial.

Haakon didn't know what to gape at first. Jens walked beside him, and when an urchin bumped into Haakon and then tried to run off, Jens stopped him, grabbing the child's hand.

"Hey! Let me go, you stinking bed bucket!"

Instead, Jens pried the child's fingers open, revealing Papa's knife! Jens released the urchin and handed the knife to Haakon.

"I told you, anything of value, you'd better keep a close watch on around here. And stay close to me. Some of these people here are worse than sharks!"

Haakon looked at the mass of people around him with a new respect, a new fear.

Haakon liked The Buccaneer Pub the minute he walked into it. It was crowded, noisy, bustling, filled with sailors from every land. Wherever Haakon turned, he heard another language — even Norwegian! Jens and Haakon joined Berg and Steine at the bar. They talked of ships and they talked of the sea.

"The sea between Sydney and Calcutta belongs to pirates. We'll earn our pay there," Berg said.

Haakon felt excited from the events of the day. He was a sailor, signed on by Captain Madsen for a long voyage. He'd made his way through the streets of London unscathed. Now, he was sitting in a sailor's pub next to some of the most experienced sailors on the seven seas. What did he care about pirates?

"Bring the pirates on! Jens has been showing me how to fight with my saber!"

"Those pirates are done for!" Jens joked. Everybody laughed, including Haakon.

The barkeep refilled Jens' mug.

"I'll be having the same," Haakon said.

The barkeep eyed him. "A pint, is it, sailor?" he asked.

Haakon nodded.

"Your special brew," Jens instructed him.

The mug was placed in front of him. Haakon took it and spoke to his mates.

"I used to be afraid of everything," he told them,

confessing to them as he could never have told any-body before. "Now, I'm not afraid of anything."

He picked up the mug and drank deeply.

The vile, sharp, pepper-flavored brew gagged Haakon. Suddenly, he couldn't swallow, he couldn't talk, he couldn't even breathe! All he could do was spit it out, every drop of it, spraying the mouthful all over the bar, all over the floor, all over himself.

His friends were roaring with laughter — es-pecially Jens and the barkeep.

Haakon knew he must have made a terribly funny sight, spurting the doctored brew everywhere. Once he could breathe again, he laughed as hard as anyone there. That was when Haakon knew he was no longer a boy. He was a man. And he was among friends who were laughing with him, not just at him.

And when he could talk once more, he sprung up onto the bar and drew his saber. He held it high above his head and spoke.

"Let the pirates beware! Today, I am a sailor!"

Jens, Berg, and Steine stood up, as did all the mates from the *Flora* who filled The Buccaneer.

The cry went up, "To Haakon! To Haakon!"

He wasn't a bit afraid.

The crew of the *Flora* lined up for inspection. They were to set sail from London within the hour. Captain Madsen had some words for them. There were two uniformed men with him. Haakon stood as tall as he knew how, back rigid, shoulders square, eyes straight ahead.

"The voyage ahead takes us to Sydney and then

to Calcutta. That, as you know, is pirate territory. The company has signed on a first mate who knows those troubled waters — Lieutenant Howell and his assistant Royal Bosun Jim Thatcher.

"Mr. Howell is one of the most respected officers in the Royal British Navy — "

Everybody knew that, Haakon thought. Howell's reputation had even reached his small town in Norway. The man had defeated more pirates than most sailors ever met.

"He saw action when the pirates were routed out of Borneo. I am pleased to have him and his bosun join us and wish him welcome. Mr. Howell?"

The captain stood back. Howell came forward. His uniform was impressive, clean and freshly pressed, with shiny brass buttons. But what Haakon noticed most was the man's face. He had sharp features, a shock of black hair, piercing gray eyes, and a long, jagged scar running the length of his right cheek.

"You're a fine-looking crew," Howell began. "I have no doubt you'll be doing your finest to make this crossing as fast as nature allows. And, as a little incentive, the company has authorized me to pay a bonus to every member of the crew, if we get to Calcutta ahead of schedule."

The crew smiled proudly. They would work hard indeed, for a bonus.

"We don't expect any trouble from pirates. His Majesty's navy has already sent most of them off to where they belong!"

Haakon was impressed that Howell didn't give

himself credit for the job. Most of the sailors on the ship knew he was the one who'd done it.

"Now, ready to cast off!"

The crew scrambled to their assigned jobs. Haakon sprinted easily up the ropes of the mainmast and helped raise the mainsail.

He was about to begin the most exciting adventure of his life, and he was ready for it!

Chapter 5

That night, Haakon was assisting the captain's steward to serve dinner to the captain, the ship's doctor Bakken, and Mr. Howell in the captain's quarters. Haakon stood immobile and silent, watching, waiting for a chance to be helpful.

The captain unlocked his private cabinet and removed a bottle of brandy.

"That announcement about the bonus took me by surprise," he told Howell.

On signal from the steward, Haakon brought three glasses, put them on the table in front of the captain, and stood back.

"The company told me about it right before I boarded," Howell said.

The captain appeared dubious. "Well, I won't push the crew, but if we get there ahead of schedule, the men will deserve a bonus. Brandy, Mr. Howell?" he asked.

"You should be honored, Mr. Howell," Dr. Bakken told him. "Captain Madsen rarely offers his personal supply to anyone."

"That's because I rarely drink," the captain explained. "Except for a glass before bed to help me sleep."

Howell took the glass the captain offered him, sniffed it curiously, and drank the whole glass down in one gulp. Haakon couldn't help noticing the looks of surprise on the faces of the captain and his doctor, who sipped slowly from their own glasses.

The captain refilled Howell's glass.

When dinner was served, Haakon saw that Howell was as ill-mannered at the table as he had been with the brandy. He crammed food into his mouth and chewed with his mouth open. Haakon's mother would have sent him to the barn to eat with the pigs if he'd eaten the same way at the family table.

Howell became aware of the stares he was getting. "I enjoy my food and drink too much to be a gentleman about it," he confessed. Then he raised his glass. "To a good voyage," he said. The captain and Bakken drank with him.

Haakon knew that Howell was a world-famous hero and pirate-fighter. He also knew that, although he might be an officer, the man was no gentleman.

Haakon felt he had learned something. It was obvious that manners had nothing to do with the ability to kill pirates.

The *Flora* headed west and then south from London, sailing along the French and then Portuguese coasts. It headed due south along the African coast, bound for the Cape of Good Hope. At that point, they would round the southern tip of Africa and leave the Atlantic for the Indian Ocean.

As the days passed, it seemed to Haakon that every day something new and exciting happened. Every day he learned, and every day he became a better sailor.

Most of the time he took his orders from the bosun, sometimes from Captain Madsen himself. And then, one day, Howell asked him to do something for him. He wanted his charts, which were stowed in the ship's hold.

Haakon carried a lantern into the dark, dank hold, searching for the pouch Howell had described. It would be hanging from a peg near some other crates marked with his personal name. . . .

"Oof!"

Haakon tripped on something or, more accurately, some*one*.

"What do you want, boy?" Thatcher growled at him. The man had been sleeping in the hold.

"Oh, sorry. Mr. Howell sent me to find his charts. He said they're in a pouch down here somewhere."

"Well, find the pouch for yourself and be quick about it!" Thatcher snapped. Then he bounded up the ladder out of the hold, leaving Haakon by himself.

The hold was filled with carefully piled crates, barrels, and bales. It took him a few minutes to locate the ones with Mr. Howell's name on them. There were seven, stacked high, and on the top of those lay Mr. Howell's pouch. Haakon set down the lantern and began scrambling up the stack. When he could reach the pouch, he grabbed it, and descended as he'd come. However, his foot caught onto something and wedged along the end of one of the crates, yanking the siding off it. Haakon slid down to the floor of the hold and tried to replace the siding. Before he did that though, he decided to satisfy his curiosity. After all, what on earth would a British naval officer need to store in seven sealed crates in the hold of a merchant ship?

Rifles. The crate was filled with them, and the six identical crates no doubt had identical contents.

"Are you still down there, boy?" Howell's voice pierced the darkness.

Haakon hurried to get the siding back on the crate. "Here, sir!" Haakon answered sharply. Howell appeared. "I found the pouch, sir," he said, handing it to Howell.

"That's a good lad," he said, smiling broadly, but Haakon knew the man could see the dislodged siding on the crate. "You've impressed me, young Haakon. You're coming into your own as a sailor."

Haakon wondered what he was getting at. He didn't like the sweetness in Howell's voice. "Thank you, sir," he said.

"And if there's a secret to be kept, for the good of the ship and her crew, well, young Haakon, any good sailor knows to keep his mouth shut, doesn't he?"

Haakon felt his mouth go dry with fear from the sweet threat in the voice. "I don't know any secrets, sir," he stuttered, feeling for all the world as if he were facing Ole by the snow-covered bank of the wide stream near his home.

"Just in case you do . . ." Howell signaled Haakon

to proceed up the ladder. Howell's voice followed him with each rung.

"I heard a tale once of a sailor who told something he shouldn't have. Half the crew was lost because of it, and the half that survived cut the sailor's tongue out and ran it up the main halyard."

Haakon nearly gagged with the horrible thought.

"Are you understanding what I'm saying, boy?"

"Yes, sir," was all Haakon could manage before he fled.

Haakon climbed up the rigging to the top of the foremast. He needed to be alone to consider what had happened in the hold, but no matter how long Haakon thought about the events, he couldn't make sense of them. All he knew for sure was that Mr. Howell was a treacherous man — far more dangerous than Ole and his bullying buddies could ever be. No wonder so many pirates had fallen by his hand.

Chapter 6

The following day brought the *Flora* into rough waters. Haakon had never felt anything like it. The ship bobbed about in the seas. Most of the sailors had been through many more storms far worse than this one, as they seemed to enjoy telling him. Without any apparent concern they went about their tasks, securing ropes and lowering the sails against the force of greater winds.

For Haakon, it wasn't so easy. It wasn't that he was frightened. He'd learned that the sailors knew what they were doing, and if they weren't worried, he wasn't, either. However, his stomach apparently hadn't gotten the news. With each new swell of waves, Haakon's stomach protested, violently. He grasped the railing and hoped that nobody was watching.

"Storm bothering you, kid?" Jens teased.

Pale and weak, Haakon looked at him. "Storm? You call this a storm?" he joked. Jens clapped him proudly on the back.

"You two!" Howell interrupted. "Secure the jib stay!"

"Aye aye, sir!" Jens said.

Haakon, however, couldn't move.

"What's the matter with you, ship's boy?" Howell demanded.

"He's sick, sir," Jens answered for Haakon.

"Everyone works on board ship, sick or not," Howell spat out.

Haakon wondered what was coming. He remembered Howell's warning.

"Is there a problem, Mr. Howell?" Captain Madsen asked.

"Captain, Haakon is — " Jens began.

"The boy's sick," Howell said. "I told him to go below."

"You heard the lieutenant, Haakon," the captain said. Haakon saluted weakly and made his way to his own hammock. He was too sick to try to understand the events. No matter how he looked at them, they didn't make sense. What he did know, though, was that he was the lowliest crew member aboard and Howell was the second-ranking officer after Captain Madsen. Like Captain Madsen, his word was law.

Later that night, the seas calmed and so did Haakon's stomach. He knew he would live when he awakened in his hammock and all he could think of was how hungry he was. The cook usually left bread and cheese in the galley for sailors with the overnight watch. Haakon wondered if there might be any there for him.

He dropped out of his hammock and made his way through the dark passageways of the ship to the galley. A lone candle burned there, lighting a small supply of bread and cheese. Tentatively, Haakon tried a crust of the bread. It went down easily and stayed down. He took another bite, this time adding some of the cheese. That, too, tasted good to him. He took out his father's knife, cut off a small portion of bread and cheese for himself and took them to the seat at the corner of the mess where he, as lowliest crew member, usually sat. He munched quietly.

The mess and galley were next to the captain's cabin, near Howell's and the doctor's. The captain's cabin door was wide open. He must be on deck at the helm, Haakon thought. While Haakon sat in the dark corner, he saw a crack of light. Howell's cabin door opened. Thatcher appeared.

The man glanced around furtively. Haakon instinctively drew into the dark corner, staying out of Thatcher's sight. Thatcher walked into Captain Madsen's cabin. Haakon squinted to see what he was doing. He saw Thatcher remove Captain Madsen's keys from his desk and turn to the captain's cabinet. Then, without making a sound, Thatcher removed a bottle of Captain Madsen's special brandy — the brew that Howell had "enjoyed" so much that first night at sea.

Thatcher "enjoyed" it, too. He "enjoyed" three

big swigs of it! Then, as Haakon watched, he poured something into the bottle. He must be watering down the brandy to hide the fact that some is missing, Haakon realized.

Haakon wondered briefly if he should tell the captain that Thatcher was filching his good liquor. Then he thought of the sailor whose story Howell had told him. What would Howell do with a ship's boy who tattled on a Royal Navy Bosun?

Haakon wished his father were there to advise him, just as he also wished his mother had been there to take care of him when he was ill. Thoughts of home welled up in his heart. He felt very alone and very afraid.

The following morning, the seas were calm and the sun was bright. Haakon was still a little weak from his sickness the day before and sad from the events and thoughts of the night before.

"Morning, lad. You're looking better," Jens greeted him. "There's no cure for two things sailors get, you know — seasickness and homesickness."

"I'm not homesick," Haakon said, but he suspected that, as usual, Jens was reading his thoughts. He was uncanny about that.

"I was talking about myself," Jens said.

"What's it like, your home?" Haakon asked.

"Just a little cabin on one of the most beautiful beaches you ever saw. I got me a fishing boat and a lady. We catch salmon to make our living. Oh, Haakon, the sunsets there, they are like the sky opened up and heaven showed through!"

"Where is it?" Haakon asked.

Jens gave him a wry smile and then tapped his finger to his temple. "Up here," he said. "It's the only place I can afford to have it — yet. But some-day, who knows?"

Haakon hoped that one day Jens would have that home. He even hoped he could help him get it. Now, however, that was a foolish thought. After all, Haa-kon was barely doing enough to help his family keep the home they already had. Once again, the home-sickness swept over him.

The more Haakon thought about some of the strange events he'd seen, the more he thought Cap-tain Madsen should know about them, too. It had been more than two weeks since he'd seen Howell's rifles, and Haakon had not been able to come up with one reason for him either to have them or to hide the fact.

. . . *any good sailor knows to keep his mouth shut* . . .

The words echoed in his head, but the facts of the situation rattled around there, too. What if the captain should know? It wasn't the same as telling a mate. Maybe the captain had to know. Maybe silence was worse than talking!

That night, Haakon found himself outside the captain's cabin door, listening to the end of a con-versation with Dr. Bakken.

". . . Still, if you ask me, there's something not right about this man. I say he's trouble."

Dr. Bakken was embarrassed that Haakon had

overheard any of the conversation. Haakon was hardly aware of it. His mind was on the conversation he was to have with the captain.

"You're still up?" the captain said.

"Yes, sir, Captain," Haakon began. "Sir, are there rules about, I mean . . ." He stammered uncomfortably. He wanted to do what was right, but he didn't know what it was.

"Spit it out, boy. Usually you have no trouble saying what's on your mind."

Haakon breathed deeply. "Well, if a mate knows something about another mate, or an officer, kind of a secret. I mean, if he knows that the officer has something on board that maybe he shouldn't, should he report this officer or not?"

The captain smiled kindly. "Has one of your mates smuggled some whiskey on board?"

"I — "

"Don't worry so much, Haakon," he said, putting his arm around Haakon's shoulders.

"I just want to be a true sailor," Haakon said.

"I've never known a truer sailor." Haakon was surprised at the compliment. "Now, for that secret of yours. You sleep on it and in the morning, if you feel you should, you come and tell me about it."

It was decided then. Haakon had just one more night to think about it and then it *would* be all right to tell.

"Yes, sir. Good night, sir," he said.

"Oh, Haakon, before you go lad, can you bring me a glass from the pantry? My steward cleaned up my brandy glass tonight before I had a chance to use it."

"Aye aye, sir."

But when morning came and Haakon returned to the captain's cabin, he once again found the doctor leaving. This time, the doctor drew the door closed tightly behind him. There was a grave look on his face.

"I need to see him," said Haakon.

"He needs a rest, lad."

Howell's cabin door opened. "How is he?" he asked Dr. Bakken.

"His temperature is high."

"Then it's ship fever," Howell said.

"Maybe, but I've never seen a ship fever attack just one man."

"He's an old man."

Dr. Bakken shook his head. He continued along the passageway. Howell turned to Haakon.

"You wouldn't be bothering the captain with any nonsense — a needless worry that could kill him?" He glared at Haakon. Haakon felt that the man's eyes could see right through him. "Aye? Because anybody who would bother the captain in this state deserves to have his tongue cut out. Aye, lad? You understand me? Because a boy needs his tongue. Without it, all he can do is scream."

"Aye aye, sir," Haakon said, fumbling to raise his hand in a salute. But Howell brushed past him and swept up a ladder onto the deck before the words were out of Haakon's mouth.

Chapter 7

Haakon stood at attention, in line with the rest of the crew. Dr. Bakken spoke.

"Captain Morgan Eiliff Madsen, we commit your remains to their final resting place. God have mercy on your soul."

Haakon was witnessing an honorable burial at sea. On signal, Captain Madsen's body, dressed in full uniform, and wrapped in the flag of his homeland, Norway, was lowered into the sea. The cannon on the side of the ship fired a final salute to the fine seaman. The crew sang a hymn.

For his part, Haakon could barely mouth the words. It seemed so impossible that the man who had told him only two days ago that he was a true sailor was now himself gone, forever. Tears welled in Haakon's eyes.

When the hymn was finished, Mr. Howell, now Captain Howell, stepped forward and addressed the crew.

"We'll all miss Captain Madsen. He was a kind man — but a poor captain." The crew glanced at one another. Not a one of them had ever sailed with a better captain than Captain Madsen. Howell continued. "We are days behind schedule, but we'll make them up. We land in Sydney tomorrow. I'm canceling shore leave for the whole crew. We stay in Sydney only long enough to load cargo, then we set sail for Calcutta."

They had been at sea for more than two months. It was hard to believe their new captain wouldn't even permit a few days in port!

"Pardon me, sir," Jens said, speaking for everyone. "We're a day ahead of our schedule, and the crew has worked hard for shore leave."

Howell glared at Jens. His gray eyes seemed to pierce the man and his long red scar almost pulsed with his anger.

"You dare talk back to an officer? This ship is now in the command of the British Navy, and we *hang* men who talk of mutiny!"

"But, sir, I wasn't — "

"Then keep your mouth shut!" Howell bellowed. His eyes darted along the line of sailors standing at rigid attention. "Anyone else have an objection to sacrificing shore leave for the good of the voyage?"

Nobody said a word. Nobody even breathed.

"Then back to work!"

They scurried back to their stations.

It wasn't easy to have the *Flora* anchored in Sydney harbor and the sailors all confined to the ship, but the crew made the best of the situation. One evening, when the work was done, a few of the men gathered on the deck to sing and share tales.

An old sailor pulled out a concertina and played a tune while a few of the men danced.

"Sydney's the kind of port that leaves a mark on a sailor," the old man mused.

"Really?" Haakon said, wondering what the man meant.

"It did on me," he said, opening up his shirt to display his chest. It was covered with tattoos! At the top, SYDNEY was printed in elaborate red and blue letters. Beneath that was an enticing selection of names and dates.

"Mary, 1838 . . . Adella, 1840 . . ." The old sailor began laughing. "Beatrice, 1843 . . . Helen, 1846." And then finally, "Mother." There was no date after "Mother."

"Mothers you love forever," he said. Everybody laughed then, including Haakon, though the thought brought some sadness to his heart. He did love his mother forever, and he missed her as well.

The next day, which was the day before they were to weigh anchor, Haakon made up his mind to share the secret of the guns with Jens. When he was sure there was no one in the hold, he took Jens down there. The siding on the crate was still loose. He jostled it a bit and removed it, revealing the contents to Jens.

Jens furrowed his brow in thought. "There could be plenty of explanations for this cargo," Jens said.

"Like what?" Haakon challenged him.

"To use against pirates," Jens reminded him.

"Maybe, but then why didn't the captain know

about them? Why are they marked 'private,' and why are they hidden?"

Jens shook his head. Haakon knew it wasn't good to question his superiors. He also knew that Jens had been scared by Howell's threat to him after Captain Madsen's funeral. Challenging Howell could be downright deadly!

"He's a British naval officer, Haakon, and he's captain now. There's rules of the sea that we have to obey, no matter how wrong they might seem. If we don't, then it's mutiny and we'll be hung. Understand?"

Before Haakon could try to answer, they both heard footsteps coming down into the hold. They slipped into the darkest corner and disappeared into the shadows.

It was Thatcher with the bosun and Steine. "Fetch two of the captain's private boxes," Thatcher ordered them. "The rest stay until we get to Batavia."

Batavia? They were supposed to go to Calcutta!

As the three men disappeared back up the ladder, Haakon and Jens exchanged looks. Something was very strange, indeed.

"Batavia's the worst of the pirates' waters," Jens said. "Taking a merchant ship there's just asking for trouble!"

"I told you, Jens. Something *is* wrong!"

There was no point in talking. There was nothing to be done. Together, the two of them returned to the deck. The last of the preparations were being made to weigh anchor. One final longboat came to the *Flora*, bringing five nasty-looking cutthroats on board.

"These are your new mates, bosun," Howell said, introducing the lot to the *Flora*'s crew.

"You didn't say anything about taking on extra crew, sir," the bosun said.

"Well, I'm saying it now!"

Chapter 8

That night, with the *Flora* bound for Batavia, the ship's cook sent Haakon down to the hold for a sack of potatoes. He made his way down the ladder and headed along an aisle formed by crates to the cook's storage bin. He picked up a small sack of potatoes.

In the dim light, he spotted movement. "Is someone down here?" Haakon asked.

There was no answer. He stood still and looked around him. At first he thought he'd been mistaken, but then he heard the unmistakable scrape of a shoe on the deck.

He followed the noise, silently dropping the sack of potatoes and removing his father's knife from his pocket. He snapped the blade out and continued forward on tiptoe in the darkness.

Suddenly he was attacked from behind. His knife skittered across the floor. Before he knew it, he was flat on his back on the floor and his attacker was sitting on his chest, covering his mouth with a hand.

"Hey, relax. Stop. I'm not going to hurt you."
The hand came off.

He blinked and found himself staring into the face of a girl about his own age.

"You're a girl!"

"You've seen one before, haven't you?" she retorted.

"Yes, I have sisters," Haakon said and then was sorry. It seemed a dumb thing to have said.

"You're kind of puny for a sailor," the girl said.

That annoyed Haakon. He pushed her off his chest and stood up. That was when he got his first good look at her.

"What are you staring at?"

"I'm not staring," he said, flustered, because, of course, he *had* been staring. "What are you doing here?"

"I'm hitching a ride to Calcutta," she said as if it were the most natural thing in the world.

"When did you get on board?"

"Sydney — "

"But why?"

"To get away from some do-gooders who want to put me in an orphanage. I'd rather take my chances with an uncle in Calcutta."

"Orphanage?"

"Yes. Both my parents died."

That was something Haakon could understand. He missed his own parents so terribly, and they were alive. It was hard to imagine how he would feel if he knew he could never see them again.

"Spare me your pity," the girl said.

"But you can't stay down here."

"I checked out your Captain Madsen. He's one of the most honorable captains at sea. Since it's too late to take me back, he'll just have to welcome me aboard."

That was when Haakon realized how much trouble the girl was in.

"You should have checked better," Haakon said. "Captain Madsen is dead."

Her face paled. "The new captain?" she asked.

"He's mean. He's horrible. He'll probably throw you to the sharks — or worse."

The two stared at one another for a few seconds. Haakon's heart went out to the orphan, and he hated to think what Howell would do to her, or anyone who helped her.

"I'll help you," he said.

"How?"

"I'll bring you food. I'll make sure I'm the only one who comes down here for supplies."

It seemed so easy to say those words, but even as they were coming from his heart, Haakon's mind was warning him that he could be getting into an awful lot of trouble himself.

"My name's Mary," the girl said.

It was a beautiful name. Suddenly the enormity of the situation, the girl in the dark and dank ship's hold for maybe months at a time, with only Haakon for a friend . . . . He gulped.

"Mine's uh — um. I'd better get you some food,"

he said quickly. He pocketed his knife, picked up his sack of potatoes, and grabbed the ladder to climb. "Haakon," he said as if he'd just remembered it. "My name's Haakon." He leapt up the last few steps, carrying in his heart forever the picture of the pretty girl named Mary in the ship's hold.

Chapter 9

The next few weeks were a confusion of good and bad. Daily, Haakon enjoyed the time he spent with his newfound friend in the hold. Daily, Howell, Royal Bosun Thatcher, and the five cutthroat sailors who joined them in Sydney made the journey more torturous for Haakon and the rest of Captain Madsen's crew.

The cutthroats were able-bodied seamen, all right. They stayed that way by hogging double rations at every meal. Thatcher did nothing to stop them. He joined them!

The five newcomers took the hammocks they wanted, throwing others' personal belongings onto the floor. Jens, Steine, Berg, and Haakon all ended up without hammocks, sleeping on the deck. Howell, usually drunk now that he had his "own" sailors to do things "his way," did nothing to help the men he'd set sail with from London.

For Haakon, the only thing that made the situation tolerable was the fact that the poor management of the ship made it easier for him to steal food, and time, for Mary.

Late at night, while the hungry and exhausted crew slept, Haakon tiptoed out of the bunk area and climbed down into the hold. On each trip, he brought the food he'd been able to steal, an apple, a potato, a chunk of meat. Whatever it was, Mary was grateful for it and ate it hungrily.

Haakon liked talking with Mary and spending time with her. He found it easy to talk with her. He was grateful that his father had taught him some English, and he found that his talks with Mary were helping him to improve it. She told him about her life in Australia before her parents died, as well as after. She showed him her most precious belonging, a book. She even offered to give it to him as thanks for saving her life.

"Why would I want a book?" he asked. "I can't read."

She seemed disappointed that he wouldn't accept her offer.

"But," he said. "You could give me something even more valuable than that. You could teach me to read."

After that, every night Haakon would bring a lantern with him when he came to give Mary food, and she would repay him by teaching him his letters and the sounds they made. Soon, he was reading.

"In Xanadu did Kubla Khan a stately . . ."

She held the lamp up high so he could make out the letters.

"Plee-ser . . ."

"Pleasure," she corrected him. He winced. "Nobody said the English language makes any sense," she joked.

". . . dome decree," he continued.

"Good."

Haakon put down the book and smiled. He appreciated her compliment. Mary took his sailor's cap and put it on her own head. Then she put it back on his.

"With that cap, you almost look like a *real* sailor," she teased. "All you need is a tattoo."

Haakon tugged the cap securely on his head. "Maybe I have one you can't see," he told her. She laughed. "What's so funny? I might have a different girl's name for every port I've been to — Helen from London, Beatrice from Sydney, Adella from — "

She giggled. "What about 'Mama'?"

Just the mention of the word *Mama* was enough to sadden Haakon and make him terribly homesick. For Mary, although it was different, it was the same. They were both silent, lost in their thoughts for a few minutes.

"What's your mother's name?" Mary asked.

"Margaret. My father calls her Maggie."

"My mother's name was Anne. Papa died first. Mama died nursing him. I hate being an orphan."

It all flooded out, almost as if it were just one sentence. Haakon knew just how she felt, and he also knew there was little he could do for her. He couldn't change the facts, so he changed the subject.

"What's Xanadu?" he asked.

"My mother said it was the most beautiful place on earth, where everyone was happy and safe. But it's just in a book. It doesn't really exist."

Haakon thought of his home. That was a Xanadu for him. And then there was the "home" Jens had in his head. That was almost as real because even thoughts of it made Jens happy.

"So this is where you've been sneaking off to every night," Jens said, as if he knew Haakon had been thinking about him.

Haakon leapt up, hitting his head on a low beam. Mary started to run in terror.

"It's okay. He's my friend!" Haakon assured her.

"Jens is my name," he said, offering his hand. She took it and introduced herself.

"A stowaway, huh?"

"She's an orphan," Haakon explained. "She has to get to a relative in Calcutta."

Jens looked back and forth between the two of them. "It's too late to tell you how foolish this is," he said. Haakon and Mary nodded. They both knew what they were doing. "Found this lying around," Jens said, opening his fist to reveal two biscuits. "I thought Haakon had smuggled a dog on board."

Mary took the biscuits and thanked him. Jens went back up the ladder and out of the hold.

"He won't tell, will he?" Mary asked.

"I trust him with my life," Haakon said, knowing it was true, and now knowing that he had to do so.

Chapter 10

Haakon was so intent on talking to Jens that he was barely aware of the motion of the *Flora* on the sea. Dark clouds built up off the port bow and the waves swelled beneath it.

"Jens," he said, approaching his friend. "Have you ever kissed a girl?"

"A few," Jens said, tugging tightly on a rope to be sure the line was secure. "And, believe it or not, some of them kissed me back — and liked it!"

"Oh," Haakon said.

"That Mary of yours isn't too hard to look at," Jens said, once again showing that he could read Haakon's mind.

"She isn't, is she," Haakon agreed, smiling.

Jens reached to check another line, found it loose, and retied the knot. "Uh-oh, these seas are starting to brew," he remarked.

Haakon looked up. Then, for the first time, he realized that what was approaching them was not just another squall. This was a storm.

The bosun appeared on deck. The rising seas had

come to his attention as well. He began shouting orders to everyone on deck. Haakon mounted the foremast, sprinted up the ladder, and secured the sail.

"Bosun!" Howell shouted rudely as he emerged from his cabin. His face was flushed with anger. "Is the ship all secure against the storm?"

"Steady as she'll be, sir," he replied.

"Then line the men up for inspection!"

"*Inspection?* Sir, we need every hand!"

"*Inspection!* You insolent dog!"

The bosun lined up every member of the crew for inspection. The captain strode back and forth in front of them, gazing at each man as he passed. Haakon felt the captain could stare right through to his soul with those eyes.

"There's a rogue among us," Howell began. "Does he have the guts to step forward and take his punishment?"

The sailors looked at one another curiously.

"Maybe I can prod your memory," he said and then nodded a signal to Thatcher.

Thatcher disappeared momentarily, and then reappeared, dragging Mary. He threw her to the deck at Howell's feet.

"We have here a stowaway. One of you has been concealing her and stealing food for her." He yanked her up by the hair. "Point out your confederates!" he shrieked.

She was silent.

Haakon knew Mary would never say anything.

What he didn't know was how long he could remain silent himself.

"Bosun, prepare to keelhaul the prisoner!" Howell shouted.

"She's only a child!" Jens protested. "You'd drown her!"

"So, it was you, Jens Gasoy!" The captain snapped an order to Thatcher. "Take her below and put her in irons. I'll deal with her later. Bosun! Get me the cat!"

Haakon had never seen the cat. He knew it was a whip with nine tails. Men had died from such whippings. He couldn't let Jens take his punishment.

"Jens didn't do anything! It was me!" Haakon said.

"Haakon!" Jens spoke sharply.

"Hold your tongue, Gasoy," Howell ordered. "Mr. Haakonsen will take his lashes like any other on this ship. Bosun, the penalty is forty strokes."

Three cutthroat sailors grabbed Haakon, tied him to the mainmast, and ripped off his shirt to bare his back for the punishment. Howell handed the whip to one of his men to do the deed.

"Sir, that cat will kill the lad. You can't do that!"

There was a wicked sparkle in Howell's eye. "I could, Mr. Gasoy," he said. "But I think that this time *you* will. Pick up the lash."

Jens didn't move. Haakon was totally overwhelmed by the events. How could it be, he wondered, that within just a few minutes everything which had seemed wonderful, was now so dreadful.

Mary in chains, himself at the mercy of Howell, and Jens on the brink of mutiny. The whole world was crashing around him.

Then as if to prove his fear, there was a crash — a real one. There was a terrible flash of light and the loudest roar Haakon had ever heard. Haakon looked up. The topmast yardarm had been broken clean off by a streak of lightning and was tumbling down to the deck through the maze of ropes and ladders.

"Sir!" the bosun yelled, pointing.

Then, to the horror of everybody, the entire foremast came crashing down, ripping ropes and ladders, tearing sails. It gained momentum as it fell, finally landing with such force on the deck that it ripped right through the boards and tore a large hole in the side of the ship.

In a matter of seconds, the *Flora* was sinking.

"Cast the longboats!" Howell ordered. The sailors broke ranks and ran for their lives.

Jens went first to Haakon. He sliced the ropes that bound him to the remaining mast. "Go after your friend!" he said urgently.

Haakon fled for the brig.

"Help me!" he heard Mary cry. "Help me!"

The water was already up to Haakon's ankles and the level was rising quickly. There was not a second to spare. Mary was imprisoned in a room locked with a heavy bolt and there was no key in sight.

He looked around for help. What he found was a bench floating past him. He picked it up and began beating at the bolt and the door with it.

"Help!" Mary kept calling.

He was trying.

On the fourth try, the bench slammed against the bolt so hard that it ripped the door out of its hinges. The door swung open.

"Haakon!" Mary said, her face filled with relief. But as soon as Haakon saw the irons that bound her hands and feet, he knew his troubles were not over.

"The key! It's on the wall!" Mary said, pointing with her bound hands.

The key was on the wall, but it was on a hook designed for a full-grown person, not a fourteen-year-old lad, and the gush of rising water made it harder still. Haakon needed help. He looked desperately at Mary. The sight of his friend with water now nearly up to her chin was all the help he needed. One more attempt and he had the keys.

It took three tries for Haakon to unlock the irons on Mary's hands and another four to undo her legs. By the time she was free, she was coughing and sputtering, trying to rid herself of the seawater that had forced its way into her lungs. The important part was that she was free.

Haakon took her hand and together the two of them fought their way through the ship and up the ladders to the deck.

Up on the deck they found Jens desperately fighting with Howell to make the longboat wait for Haakon and Mary.

"Damn you, Gasoy!" Howell bellowed. "Release the boat!"

Jens held on for dear life — his, Haakon's, and Mary's.

"Pull him in!" Howell ordered.

With that, Howell's cutthroat sailors slashed the ropes holding the longboat and it splashed down into the wild sea, pulling Jens along with it. Haakon and Mary ran to the side.

"Jens!" Haakon yelled.

Jens struggled through the rough sea, holding onto the chain that was his only hope for safety. Howell ignored his pleas. He ordered his men to row away from the *Flora* before she went down.

Haakon understood two things. He understood that he and Mary and Jens would only survive if he did the right thing. He also understood that there was no room for fear in his heart.

Almost without thinking, he began to act. He untied a rope from the mainmast and began throwing it to Jens. Mary held him by the waist so he could reach farther, but each throw seemed more and more futile. Finally, a wave rolled over Jens and pulled him under the water. The same wave swept up onto the deck of the *Flora* and swept Haakon and Mary away from the edge of the ship. The deck tilted even more dangerously. They had to go, or they would go down with it.

There was one boat left, a small rowboat, hardly the vessel for rough waters like these, but it was the only chance. Haakon took Mary's hand and helped her crawl toward it. The rowboat was lashed to the side of the ship. Haakon lifted Mary up and

then lowered her over the side into the little life-boat. He prepared to follow her.

The *Flora* lurched. A wave washed over the hull and swept across the tilted deck. As if he were a piece of driftwood, the water picked Haakon up and carried him straight off the ship and into the black and churning waters below.

He fought and struggled, kicking and flailing his arms. Finally, he rose to the surface and gasped for air before another wave hit him and carried him still farther away from Mary.

The rain began pelting from above. He heard the groan of wood as the *Flora* sank, but he could see nothing.

"Mary! Jens!" he cried.

Another wave hit him. And then he could feel nothing.

Chapter 11

Haakon opened his eyes slowly. He was only vaguely aware of his discomfort, bruises, cuts, thirst, and hunger. What struck him most was the fact that he wasn't moving. The motion of the sea had stopped. He looked around. He wasn't on the sea anymore. He was lying on a beach, pinned down by a heavy wooden door. The small patch of sand where he lay was bordered by a bleak rocky landscape, dotted with scrawny failing palm trees.

"Oh," he said, realizing simultaneously both that he was not dead and that he might as well be.

He slithered out from under the wooden door which, he reasoned, had probably saved his life. He had a slight recollection of grabbing for something to hold onto in the storm-tossed ocean. That must have been it.

Haakon sat up. He examined himself. He found the cuts and bruises which hurt him, but knew immediately that none of them was serious. Somehow, he had been saved, but for what?

His hand went to his pocket to feel for his father's knife. It was not there. Panicked, he jumped up and looked around, searching desperately for the good-luck charm his father had given him.

To his right, something glinted in the harsh, beating sun. Haakon ran the few feet. There, almost covered by the sand, was the knife. He picked it up, opened the blade, cleaned the sand and grit off it, and returned it to his pocket. Haakon felt that somehow, as long as he had the knife, he would be okay. He could make it.

Haakon looked around. He saw nothing but rocks and spindly palm trees. He heard the loud cawing of birds and saw them flying above him, but they held little promise for him.

"Jens! Mary!" he cried, hoping against hope that the wave that pulled Jens down had released him and that the one that had swept him overboard had spared Mary. Remembering the storm, Haakon realized what faint hopes those were. He had no idea where the *Flora* had sunk or how far he'd traveled in the night before being washed up — or even if it had only been one night.

"Mary! Jens!"

The only answer was the irritated caws of the birds on the rocks above him. It was worse than silence.

Haakon realized then that he was very hungry. He set off to explore the island and find something to eat.

He found that it was a small island and none of it was any more inviting than what he'd seen in the first place. There were a few patches of scraggly vegetation, but no fruit trees or berries. The only inhabitants of the island were the birds, and their constant cawing was a warning, not an invitation.

Haakon crawled up the rocks and discovered the reason for the racket the birds were making. The island was their breeding area. The cliff was covered with nesting mothers. And, Haakon reasoned, if they were nesting, there were eggs beneath them. A thousand birds shrieked from their nests. Surely they could spare one egg for a hungry boy.

Haakon approached the closest nest cautiously. When he was three feet from it, a bird swooped down from above and began to peck at Haakon viciously.

"Yeoooow!" Haakon shielded himself with his arm and backed away helplessly. These birds weren't kidding!

He tripped and tumbled backwards, right into another nest guarded by even more vicious birds.

As fast as he could, Haakon stood up and ran, abandoning all hope of stealing an egg from the birds. Even if it could be done, it wouldn't be worth the risk of his life.

He continued climbing on the rocks, hoping to find something, but there was nothing. The only thing he learned from his climb was the knowledge that the little island offered no hope for survival. Haakon was as alone as a person could be, surrounded by a hostile world of birds and rocks. Ringing that were miles and miles of empty blue —

Then Haakon blinked. He thought he saw something. He squinted and shaded his eyes and looked again. It didn't go away. There, way across the water, was another island. It wasn't rocky and hostile. It wasn't populated by screeching birds on rocky ledges. It was green and hilly, large and lush. It was an island a boy could live on — if he could get to it.

Haakon studied the distance. It was a mile, perhaps two. In these waters, though, it might as well be a thousand, Haakon thought. For even as he looked across the way, he could see the calm waters cut by the dorsal fins of the sharks who inhabited them. If he could swim, which he couldn't, he'd never make it. He'd have to have a boat, a sturdy one, and he had nothing.

Haakon retreated to the beach. The sunset brought a cool evening breeze with it. Haakon shivered. He clawed through the sand, hoping to find something to eat or drink. He spotted some dry seaweed. Without hesitating, he put it into his mouth and gulped it down, trying to ignore the vile taste. It came back up as fast. This wasn't food.

The wind blew again. Haakon wrapped his arms around himself trying to get warm, but the breeze cut right through his thin shirt.

Desperately seeking something to comfort himself, he gathered a small collection of dry palm fronds. He piled them on the beach and tried striking his father's knife against a rock to make a spark that might start a fire. He managed to get a few sparks, but they were not enough to ignite the palms.

Haakon finally gave up. He lay down on the damp sand and slept fitfully.

He dreamed of coming home to a beautiful, fruitful, welcoming Norway. He saw his family farm in front of him. He ran to it. When the door opened, though, what came out were angry shrieking birds, clawing and pecking at him. He awoke to the cold, dark reality of his isolated island with a start, his face covered with tears.

"Jens! Mary!" he cried to the black night. There was no answer.

When morning came, Haakon's eyes turned immediately to the lush green island across the waters. He knew that if he was going to survive, it would be there, not here. This island, which had saved his life, would not sustain it. Even the sharks that separated the two islands offered more hope than the barren rocks and their hostile birds.

Haakon set to work. He lugged the trunks of two fallen palm trees to the small beach. Using every bit of vine he could cut with his father's knife, he tied the wooden door that he'd ridden from the *Flora* between the long tree trunks. When he was sure it was as secure as he could make it, he pushed his makeshift raft into the shallow water.

It stayed together and it floated. There wasn't much more that could be said about it. Water washed over the door that would be his deck. The trees were too big to cut with his knife. It was awkward, but it floated and might offer some safety from the sharks in the water.

Haakon picked up a large piece of driftwood. It would serve as his paddle. Carefully he mounted the raft, centered himself on it, and pushed off.

The sea was calm and the gentle breeze was at his back. The water, almost invisible beneath him, revealed the richness of the sea. Small and medium-sized fishes swarmed beneath him. As he paddled, he imagined how he would make a spear to catch fish for himself. He could almost smell them cooking on a warm fire. Haakon felt a glimmering of hope.

The first sign of trouble came when Haakon realized that his raft was taking on more and more water. The tree trunks were so rotten that they were absorbing the seawater and would soon sink, pulling the door, Haakon, and his paddle with them. Haakon began to paddle harder. The island was close now, perhaps no more than two hundred yards.

There was a thump. The raft came to a halt. It had lodged itself on a coral reef just a few inches beneath the water. Haakon used his bare foot to lift his craft off the obstacle.

"Yeoch!" he cried, realizing that he'd cut his foot on the sharp coral. He pulled it back and examined it. It was bleeding badly, but the cut wasn't deep. Haakon had enough experience with wounds to know that although it looked bad, it wasn't serious. He could take care of it when he got to the island. He dipped the bleeding foot into the cool seawater, hoping to ease the pain. Then he picked up his paddle and resumed his voyage.

There was another, more violent jolt to the raft, and this time it wasn't coral. It was a shark!

Haakon watched as the creature's dorsal fin whizzed past the raft, reversed direction, and attacked again.

It was the blood. Haakon knew it. The shark had smelled the blood from his wounded foot and had followed the scent to find him.

Haakon wanted to scream, but he knew it wouldn't do any good. There was no one to hear him. There was no one to save him. This was between Haakon and the shark.

The shark attacked from below this time, upending the waterlogged raft and tossing Haakon into the sea. Haakon held onto his paddle and swung at the attacking beast. The paddle splintered uselessly. Haakon was on his own.

Using every ounce of his dwindling energy he swished around in the water, searching for anything that would offer safety. He found the coral reef. He scrambled onto it, ignoring the cuts and scratches it caused. He drew his legs out of the water and crawled to safety at the center of the reef where the shark could not reach him.

He gasped for breath. Shivers of fear racked his body. He knew he couldn't let the fear take over.

"No," he told himself, speaking out loud so he could hear his own voice. "I can do it. I *will* do it."

The shivers ceased then. Haakon watched the water for more signs of the shark. When he was sure it was gone and would not return, Haakon bound his bleeding foot with his shirtsleeve and made his way as best he could to the island.

The warm sand and lush vegetation were all the welcome he needed.

He picked up a rock, threw it at a coconut high above him, and caught the fruit when it dropped from above. Haakon cracked it on a boulder. The fruit split open, revealing a pungent pulp and a cache of sweet coconut milk, which he downed in a few thirsty gulps.

Haakon knew then that he would survive.

Chapter 12

When Haakon had eaten three more coconuts and four bananas, he was ready to begin exploring the island — for water. He was certain that an island with such lush vegetation must have a water supply. He walked inland, making mental notes of other fruit trees for future meals.

"Jens! Mary!" he shouted. There was no answer. The island, it seemed, could provide everything for him but his friends.

Before long he discovered a pool of fresh water, fed by a stream that surged down from the mountain above. Haakon fell onto his stomach by the edge of the pool and drank deeply from the cool clean water. Then when he'd had his fill, he pulled off his soiled and tattered clothes and jumped into the cool water. He stood under the waterfall and allowed the water to tumble down onto him.

Every drop of the fresh water seemed to ease the pains in his battered body and in his heart.

When he was clean and refreshed, he washed his filthy clothes and then put them back on to dry. He lay in the sun on a rock and relaxed for the first time since Captain Howell and the storm had changed his life.

Haakon considered his situation. It wasn't as bad as it might have been. Now that he'd gotten to this island, Haakon could live indefinitely on the bounty of the land. He could probably make a home for himself. With his father's knife, he'd be able to carve a spear and catch some of the bounty of the sea.

There was just one thing he would not have: company. He would be alone, totally by himself, until a ship came by and found him.

"Mary! Jens!" he cried out.

There was no answer.

Haakon napped in the sun. When he woke up, it was evening and he was hungry again. He returned to some of the fruit trees he'd spotted on the way to the pond, and once again filled himself with their goodness. He lay on the soft sand, still warm from the tropical sunshine, and he slept.

In the morning, Haakon began his serious examination of the whole island. It wasn't a big island, perhaps a mile wide and two miles long. Most of the interior of the island was covered with the dense foliage of a rain forest that grew on the mountain in the center of the island.

He began by walking along the beach until he came to a rocky cliff that rose straight up from the sea. Haakon followed it inland and found himself walking through a deep ravine, cut right into the mountain. It was an extraordinary place. The ravine was about twenty feet wide, and the mountain rose on either side of it so that Haakon was walking between two walls of sheer rock, covered by masses of vines that seemed to drip from above. He tugged at the vines. They were as strong as rope. That gave Haakon some ideas. After all, he'd spent months on a ship, learning everything there was to know about ropes.

Haakon climbed up the rocky hillside of the mountain, making his way through the forest. It was as if he'd walked into another world. Suddenly, the gentle calm of the seashore was behind him. The dark, moist air of the rain forest surrounded him completely. He took a step. A stick snapped beneath his foot. The forest came alive. From everywhere, there were sounds. Birds called loudly. Bats flapped all around him. Animals he'd never heard before shrieked messages of warning.

"Jens! Mary! Anybody!!!!"

There was no answer.

Haakon looked around in fear and, finding no help, no answer, he turned to run. There was a vine in front of him. He reached forward to push it out of his way. It hissed and pushed back.

"Yeooooo!!" Haakon bellowed, releasing the snake. He fled the dark forest as fast as he could and, when he could feel the sun on him, he knew he was free of it. He sat down on his knees, breathing hard.

When his heart stopped thumping, he considered what had just happened. A picture came to Haakon's mind. It was a picture of a boy who had survived a shipwreck, outfoxed a shark, and found a place to live but who was, nevertheless, as scared of a flapping bat and an annoyed snake as he had once been of a bully named Ole.

Haakon suddenly realized how foolish he must have looked. He wished Jens were there to laugh at him, and Steine and Berg — even the bosun. He began laughing at himself. At first, the sounds of his own laughter echoing through the ravine seemed lonely, but then, hearing them come back at him, he knew that those were good sounds, not lonely ones. He laughed deeply and heartily, enjoying it, even by himself.

Haakon stood up then and continued his exploration. He'd noticed a cave halfway up the wall of the ravine. Since he'd decided to leave the jungle at least for the day, he returned to the ravine to explore the cave.

Vines hung down across the entrance to the cave, sweeping the floor of the ravine. Haakon took one and tested its strength. It seemed all right. He hoisted himself up, inching his way toward the entrance to the cave, twenty feet above the ravine floor.

His arms had been strengthened by his months at sea. Climbing up a wall with the help of a strong rope was not difficult for the able-bodied ship's boy of the *Flora*. When his head was level with the floor of the cave, Haakon peered in. It was a big cave. He could see that it went way back into the mountainside. It was the kind of place a man could use as a shelter, Haakon thought.

Then Haakon realized that the cave was the kind of place a man *had* used. Haakon was staring directly at a small leather pouch, wedged between two rocks.

"Oh!" Haakon said. At that instant, the vine snapped and Haakon tumbled to the floor of the ravine and landed in the soft sand.

Without hesitation, Haakon tested a few of the remaining vines, selected the strongest one, and once again mounted the wall. This time, he heaved himself up onto the shelf of the cave and entered it.

It was as big as he'd thought, maybe even bigger. The shadows lengthened as Haakon went further into the cave, exploring cautiously. He'd already had enough run-ins with bats and snakes for one day.

He took one step after another slowly, feeling ahead with his hand in the darkness. His arm swept into a large spiderweb. The sticky strands clung to him. He shook his arm and tried to wipe the threads off on the rock and then on his own trousers. He lost his balance and tripped as he stepped forward. There was a noisy clattering when he landed.

Haakon squinted in the dim gray light of the cave and found himself staring straight into the unmistakable hollow eyes of a human skeleton.

For the second time that day, Haakon went running away, screaming, from his explorations.

Chapter 13

Haakon approached exploring the cave more sensibly the second time. First he built himself a small fire at the cave's edge, and he made a torch with a stick and some green vines that would burn slowly. He made a weapon by tying his father's knife to the end of another stick and secured the weapon to a loop at the waist of his trousers so he couldn't drop it. Then, lighting his torch, he entered the cave.

He soon found the skeleton that had frightened him so, and the noose from which the poor man had been hanged. A few feet beyond he found another skull, this one broken in two. Haakon began to feel that his venture into the cave was raising more questions than it was answering. Nonetheless, he continued.

He was prepared when the bats, disturbed by his torch, fled, flapping their wings and soaring through the hollow mountain. Haakon dropped to the floor of the cave and lay there until they had passed. When he was standing up, however, he noticed that the floor in front of him was completely covered with leaves and branches. It seemed odd. He pushed them aside on a hunch that they were simply there to cover something. He found his hunch was correct.

The branches covered a pit. It was a trap — laid by whom? Why?

More questions. Fewer answers.

He tossed a pebble into the pit to see how deep it was. There was a long wait and then a faint splash. Haakon was more than a little relieved that he'd discovered the trap in time. He had no desire to have his bones join those of the skeletons who already inhabited the cave.

He proceeded cautiously, moving backward from the pit. Suddenly Haakon felt the floor give way under him and he slid helplessly over the edge of a second pit. He scrambled to get hold of something. His arms flailed, releasing his torch. The torch tumbled downward in the darkness until it hit the water below and went dark. Haakon tumbled after it.

And then he suddenly stopped. Somehow, his makeshift weapon, tied to a loop on his trousers, had become lodged between two rocks and was holding him suspended above the deep pit.

Slowly, carefully, knowing that his life depended on caution, Haakon pulled himself up by the spear. Inch by inch, he proceeded, feeling the strain of his weight, remembering how the vine had snapped on him before. This would be no soft landing in a sandy bed!

Finally he reached the top, found a rock that would hold his weight, and pulled himself out completely. When he was sure he was on hard cave floor, free of all hidden traps, he lay down, gasping with relief.

When he recovered, Haakon returned to the mouth of the cave, fashioned a new torch for himself, and returned far more slowly and cautiously to the cave. He greeted the skeleton and skull with new respect as he passed them this time.

There was a part of Haakon that thought it a foolish risk to attempt to study the cave anymore. Surely there would be other booby traps and pits. Deeper, however, there was a part of Haakon that knew that anybody who went to such great trouble to protect something had something valuable to protect. Haakon had to find out what that something was.

There was something at the back of the cave against the wall. In fact, as Haakon saw it, there were three things. He approached slowly, feeling the floor in front of him, looking for traps on the walls and ceiling. There were no more. He crawled to the rear of the cave and then looked, just looked.

There, in front of him, were three large sea chests. He could not know what was in them, but on top of one of them was the biggest silver bowl Haakon had ever seen.

Chapter 14

It took Haakon only a few minutes to find the tool he needed to remove the chests from the cave. He spotted a few long and strong pieces of wood and he used them to make tracks upon which to pull the chests. It was slow and hard going, but it worked. By evening, all three chests stood at the mouth of the cave. The silver bowl and a few other pieces of silver he'd found scattered about were there as well.

The chests were bolted closed with large padlocks. Not surprisingly, there was no sign of a key. There were, however, plenty of big rocks. Haakon took a few of them and pounded at the metal. Weakened and corroded by long exposure to salt air and water, the lock soon broke open.

Haakon lifted the heavy lid of the first chest. The chest was filled with more silver, bowls, platters, cups, mugs, and cutlery. Even years of neglect and tarnish couldn't hide the fact that this one chest had more silverware in it than Haakon had ever seen before in his whole life. That silver would have bought his family farm several times over!

Haakon sat back, astonished. The mysterious cave still seemed to deliver two questions for every answer it offered.

Haakon picked up the stone and hacked some more. The second chest didn't have silver in it. It was filled with gold. There were gold coins from every country Haakon had ever heard of, and from plenty he hadn't.

The third chest was even more astonishing. The first thing Haakon saw was a jewel-handled saber. He pulled it out and gaped at it. Removing it from its scabbard, he tested the fine steel blade and found it sharp as a razor. The silver, gold, and jewels were valuable in a world outside of Haakon's island. To him, the saber was the greatest treasure of all because he could use it right where he was.

The third chest held other treasures, though, and when Haakon finally put aside the saber, he returned his attention to it. The next thing he found were dozens of leather pouches, just like the one he'd seen at the mouth of the cave. These were filled with gunpowder. There were also bullets and a pistol. Beneath that, there were four long knives, a broadsword with some odd pictures on it that looked like what one of the sailors had described as Chinese writing. The chest also held silk scarves, jeweled necklaces, rings, earrings, and tiaras. Haakon smiled, thinking how beautiful Mary would be with these, and how much she would love them.

He removed the final silk scarf and discovered the other great treasure the chest held for him: a spyglass.

It didn't look much like the captain's spyglass on the *Flora* because it was covered with jewels: blue, red, green, even white. But it wasn't the jewels that thrilled Haakon. He opened it, just as he'd seen Captain Madsen do hundreds of times, and held it up to his right eye.

It took a minute for Haakon to get used to what he was seeing, for things far away were suddenly close and things close were suddenly blurred. When he could see properly and focus it for himself, he realized that he'd be able to see his whole island at once. With the spyglass he'd be able to spot a nearby ship, even miles off, in time to set off a signal for them. The spyglass alone could be his saving.

Unable to resist temptation, Haakon tied one silk scarf about his waist, another around his head. He put two long knives and the pistol in his silk sash, a ruby necklace around his neck, diamonds on his fingers. He considered putting the tiara on his head, but dismissed the idea. It was too silly for him, mighty and fearless King Haakon of, of — what was the name of the island? — Haakon Island, of course.

He picked up his new saber and held it high. "I dub thee Haakon Island!" he declared and then brought the saber down hard on the land he'd claimed for himself.

It didn't take long then for Haakon to master the use of the saber as a spear for fish. By nightfall he'd caught two in the shallow water of a tidal pool. He lit a fire on the beach, perched one of the silver bowls on its coals, filled it with water, and made himself a fish stew, flavored with coconut milk. Haakon ate every bite and knew it was the best meal he'd had in a very long time.

His stomach full, he lay back on the warm sand, and looked up at the starry sky above. Haakon knew he had everything he would need to make it. There was no more doubt. There were many tools he could use, but survival wasn't in question anymore. He wondered if that was true for his friends. Jens, Mary —

"In Xanadu did Kubla Khan/A stately pleasure dome decree. . . ."

The sound of Haakon's own voice seemed odd in the wilderness of his island. He continued talking to his realm.

"And what is Xanadu, Mary? Somewhere magical, somewhere safe. Somewhere . . ."

Where?

Chapter 15

Over the next few days, Haakon made many more wonderful discoveries about Haakon Island. He cut a swath through the mountain jungle to find the highest point of the island. He was no longer afraid of the birds, the bats, even the snakes. This was now his island, and he knew he would live on it until the opportunity came to leave it. He would leave it then without regret. Until then, he would live on it without fear.

Standing on the top of the highest hill, Haakon opened his spyglass to survey his adopted world.

From his vantage point he could see everything. He saw, for instance, that although he was on the highest piece of land, there was a tree that rose higher still. It was a big old tree that Haakon had passed on his way up. At the base of its trunk, Haakon had discovered a hole and, upon looking in, found that the base of it was totally hollowed out. It looked like a gigantic room.

Beyond the tree, Haakon looked at the rest of the vegetation on the island and confirmed that there were enough fruit trees to feed him forever. That was in sharp contrast to the rocky island he'd left behind him. Haakon took a look at that, too. It looked no better from two miles away than it had from up close.

Haakon turned and squinted through the telescope. Far away in the other direction, farther even than the rocky island, he spied another island. This one, like his own, was lush and green. He wondered if it was possible that any of his mates had landed there. He pledged to look at it daily for signs of life.

Haakon looked in the waters closer to home. He first noticed that he didn't see any sharks. That was good news. There was, however, something very large and dark jutting out of the water near the beach on the far side of his island. Haakon adjusted the distance focus on the spyglass. He didn't believe his eyes.

There, just off the coast of his island, was the wreckage of a ship! He scanned the sight, looking for a hint, hoping it might be his own ship. Then he saw three letters that answered his wishes. F-L-O-

It was the *Flora*!

Haakon ran down the rocky mountain, followed his trail through the rain forest, and made his way as fast as he could to the wreckage of his ship.

The *Flora* lay on her side. Pieces of the ship were scattered all over the beach and in the shallow water of Haakon Island.

Haakon poked through the wreckage and began to think he'd found treasure greater by far than the chests he'd discovered in the cave.

Boxes and barrels, once safely stowed in the hold, were now scattered everywhere. They were cracked open, pouring their contents into the water and onto the sand. There were tools, pots, pans, cooking utensils, even food! Haakon discovered a crate of potatoes and cans and jars of pickles and preserves. Having potatoes even meant he'd be able to grow them for himself and have potatoes forever — if it took that long.

Then he saw something sticking out of the sand. It was small and brown. It was a leather-bound book, damaged by the sea, but still whole.

Haakon picked it up and opened it carefully. The name in the front was blurred but legible. It read *Mary Smith*.

The memory gave him joy and saddened him at the same time. He had her book. He just wished he knew she was all right.

This was no time for sentimentality. Haakon realized he would have to work quickly to salvage everything usable from the *Flora* before the sea destroyed it or washed it away. He got to work.

Over the next few days, Haakon worked as he'd never worked before. He built a small raft from planks of wood and empty water barrels and used it to haul cargo from the ship to the cove near the hollow tree he'd decided to make into his home. There was a small stream of water at the cove that he could use to navigate the raft almost all the way to the base of the tree.

Once all the salvage had been collected, Haakon

set about to make himself a home. It was hard work, but if there was one thing Haakon had, it was time.

Haakon began by creating a lift for himself from the ropes he'd collected. He took all the blocks and pulleys from the ship and made a platform, something like the plank he and Jens had used on the *Flora*. He made a lookout post for himself like the ship's crow's nest at the top of his tree, from which he could see for miles in every direction.

He stowed all his salvage in the hollowed-out tree, making one section his workshop, another his sleeping space. It was snug, it was safe, and it was his — once he'd convinced the chattering, irritated monkey who'd been hanging out there that it would be to the monkey's best advantage to leave. Blowing the ship's horn had done the trick for the poor frightened creature.

Haakon hung brass lanterns with candles in them on the walls so that he could see at night. Crates and barrels served as tables, and a scrap of sail made Haakon's hammock. Haakon had even found the old sailor's concertina. He couldn't make much music with it but, he reminded himself, he would have plenty of time to learn.

When his home was cozy and well stocked, Haakon decided to bring the chests from the cave so he could have those goods at hand. He took his small raft over to the beach by the ravine and, using more ropes and pulleys, lowered the chests to the sand.

He studied the situation. It would be difficult to take a full chest on the little raft, he decided. He'd have to empty the contents and take the booty in separate loads. He began with the chest of gold coins. He removed the coins by the handful and put them into bags made of salvaged sailcloth, placing them carefully on the raft for balance.

While he was filling the third bag, however, he discovered that the chest contained something else. His fingers found cloth. He tugged at the cloth and unfolded it. It was a large black flag, adorned only by a skull and crossbones!

Haakon realized that he shouldn't have been surprised. He should have figured out by then that this was a pirate's booty. He laughed at his own innocence, to have missed the obvious.

Then, wondering what else he might have missed, he fished down among the coins with his hands, looking for other answers.

He was not disappointed. There was a large packet of papers, wrapped in linen, discolored by age. Carefully, Haakon unfolded the linen and examined the contents.

First, there was a dagger, studded with diamonds. The name Merrick was inscribed on its blade. Haakon knew that Merrick was the most feared and despised pirate on the seven seas. Was it possible that he'd actually found Merrick's cache? Haakon looked further.

The linen, it turned out, was actually a chart of islands.

"Crocodile Island, Crab Island, Island of Fear," he could make out, realizing that that could be the group of islands where he was, including Haakon

Island! He set that aside to study later. He picked up the final pieces of paper.

They were a collection of newspaper articles about pirate attacks and terror. There was a drawing included in one of the articles. Haakon recognized the face immediately by its sharp features, piercing eyes, and the jagged scar on the man's right cheek. It was Captain Howell. But that wasn't what the article said. The article identified the man as, "John Merrick, the most feared pirate in the world!"

It sank in quickly because it was the final answer to the final question. The man who had called himself Howell wasn't Howell at all. He was Merrick! Merrick had somehow gotten Howell's orders and his uniform and had masqueraded as an officer of the royal navy. Haakon and his shipmates had served as crew to the most heartless pirate known to man!

It explained a lot. That explained the guns which would no doubt have been used eventually to overcome the ship's crew. It explained "Howell's" real fear that Haakon would tell. A more experienced sailor — like Captain Madsen — would have known immediately that there was something very wrong. And that, Haakon feared, also explained Captain Madsen's sudden and mysterious illness and death. Was it possible that Haakon had actually witnessed the murder when he'd seen Thatcher pour something into the captain's brandy?

Yes, he told himself. It was possible. For there was no doubt now that Captain Madsen's death had been no accident. He'd been murdered by Merrick!

Everything was clear now. The only remaining

question was what difference did it make to a boy stranded, perhaps forever, on an island in the middle of no place?

He picked up the next bag of gold coins and put them on the raft. It was time to get back to work.

Chapter 16

Once the treasure was stowed in the hollow tree, Haakon's home was complete. It was livable, even comfortable. The goods from the *Flora*, the tools, the food, meant he could live on Haakon Island indefinitely. He sat in a sort of throne he'd created by piling the three sea chests onto one another and surveyed all he had accomplished. He was pleased with himself.

His eyes lit on the newspaper clipping about Merrick, which he'd posted on the wall of his home. He thought about the treacherous, determined man who had threatened him every day on the *Flora*. Merrick had nearly killed him his last day on board. Haakon considered the irony of the fact that his life had been saved by the storm that had taken Merrick's.

Or had it?

The last time Haakon had seen Merrick, he and his crew of cutthroats as well as a few of the sailors from the *Flora* were rowing away from the *Flora* quite safely in a longboat. Haakon really had no idea where he had been or how long he'd been at sea before he'd washed ashore. For all he knew, Merrick was alive and well somewhere. One thing was certain: If Merrick was alive, one day he would return for his treasure.

There were many things Haakon couldn't protect, but he *could* protect himself, and he could protect the treasure, and he could do it a lot better than Merrick had with his ill-disguised pits in the cave. He could booby-trap the entire island. The following morning he set about to do just that.

The first booby trap Haakon rigged was right next to his tree house. He took a large copper pot, filled it with stones, and hoisted it high above the path that led to the tree. He then put a load of gunpowder on the dry ground below the pot, and set a silver platter from the pirate's treasure chest on top of it. He tripped the vine that held the copper pot. It came tumbling down, landing on the silver platter, which caused the gunpowder to explode. There was a hole two feet deep where the platter had been.

"Genius," he told himself, refilling the hole and resetting the trap.

Next he pulled four young palm trees across another path leading to the tree, yanking them down to the ground where he joined them with a piece of sturdy sailcloth. He camouflaged the mechanism and was about to test it by throwing a coconut at it when a volunteer came along instead. It was the monkey Haakon had shooed out of the tree. The monkey chattered as he trotted along the path. Haakon didn't want the little creature to hurt himself. He tossed the coconut at the monkey to save him from tripping the trap. The monkey picked up a stick and threw it back at Haakon. Haakon laughed at the monkey's gumption, but found that he had to cover his face to keep safe from the barrage. The monkey hopped up onto the trunk of one of the palms, looking for other things he could throw at Haakon. He spotted some tempting sticks on the ground and bounded right onto the trap.

It worked. All four tree trunks were released at once, flying up and taking the monkey with them. He whizzed past Haakon, an astonished look on his face. Eventually the trees reached their full height, and the sailcloth was stretched among them like a big tent. The monkey, however, was still flying. He'd been tossed another ten feet in the air above the trees!

He was in his element, though. As he began his descent, the monkey reached out confidently, grabbed onto a branch, and stopped his fall. Then, rather than throwing anything else at Haakon, he fled. Haakon laughed and reset the trap.

Haakon then decided to protect the cave with a booby trap, too. He returned to the ravine. First, he selected a strong vine to use to scale the wall to the cave. Then he notched the vine slightly with his father's knife so he'd know which one to use. Merrick would not know the sign and would, instead, take one of the other vines which Haakon booby-trapped by fastening them to boulders above. When tugged, the vines would merely dump the heavy load on the pirate below.

Haakon's final booby trap used the anchor of the *Flora*. Haakon suspended it in a strong tree and set the trap so that a passerby who tugged at the vine on the ground below it would be hit with the heavy anchor.

When Haakon was satisfied that his island was secure, he began work on his next project — a boat. Shipbuilding was an ancient and honorable industry, about which Haakon Haakonsen, farmer boy, knew nothing. He did, however, figure out that he could make a waterproof vessel, if he could make one without seams. That meant hollowing out a log.

The very next day he began by chopping down a tree. It was long and difficult work to clean the log and prepare it for transformation into a boat. It would take even more work to make it into a boat. The days passed, and the months, too, Haakon thought, though he really had no idea how long he'd been on the island. He only knew that if he stopped working and merely waited, he would be waiting only to die.

Determined to find a way to save himself and return to civilization, he worked even harder to hollow out the log.

Eventually, the day came when the log was hollow enough to try to put to sea. Haakon dragged it down the sandy beach to the water. He pushed it free of the sandbar and hopped in. It immediately turned over, dumping him into the ocean.

Disgusted, he stood up, righted the boat, and tried again. The same thing happened.

Dismayed, Haakon pulled it back onto the beach.

He picked up the paddle he'd carved for himself and began beating his dugout canoe with it, as if to punish it. Disappointed, angry, exhausted, Haakon finally dropped down into the sand next to his failed boat and cried.

Because of his determination to survive, Haakon hadn't let himself feel anything for months and now all the accumulated feelings came over him in a rush. He began crying, wailing, howling. Tears streaked down his face, dropped to his chest, and ran in rivulets onto the sand, the neverending sand.

When the tears subsided, Haakon slept, dreaming, as he had not for a long time, of Norway, family, farm, glistening white snow, horses, sleds, hot bread . . .

"Mama!" he cried out loud, sitting bolt up and awakening himself. "Mama!"

He opened his eyes suddenly. His mother wasn't there. Nobody was. Just a little monkey.

Then, as if the creature understood what Haakon needed, he reached out and brushed a tear from the boy's cheek. And that made Haakon cry all the harder.

When morning came, Haakon pulled his boat up off the beach and stored it under some vines. He couldn't bear the thought that all the work had gone for nothing but, for now, he had no need for a boat. He had no place to go. Nobody to go with. He shook his head at his own foolishness and got on with his life.

The days passed, becoming weeks which in turn became months. Every day his time on the *Flora* became more distant. His home seemed more un-real. He tried to imagine what his family was doing, how their life was going, but it became harder and harder to remember what it was all like.

His routine didn't vary much from day to day. He walked around Haakon Island, gathering food for himself. He swam in the cove, made safe from sharks by the reef that surrounded it. Then he washed in the fresh water of the pool. The days melted into one another, easy and comfortable. Yet something was missing and Haakon never forgot it. He was lonely.

One evening, as usual, he cooked himself some dinner in the little galley he'd set up by the creek near his tree house. He put his food on the wooden trencher that served as his plate, mounted his plank, and rose majestically to the top of his tree where he could eat his dinner, survey his world, and watch the sunset.

He took a bite of the fried fish and potatoes, drank his cool fresh water, and looked around him. It looked just the way it always did. The island, the scattered remains of the *Flora* below, the distant island beyond —

Haakon squinted. Something was different. He'd seen something, but it seemed impossible. It looked like smoke from the distant island. He opened up his spyglass and focused it carefully. It took only a minute for Haakon to make sure that he was right. There was smoke curling up from the island. And where there was smoke, there would almost certainly be people cooking on the fire that produced it.

Haakon could feel his heart beating with the excitement. He abandoned his dinner, slid down his rope lift, and began foraging through his collected salvage. There had been rockets on board the *Flora*. He took one to the mountaintop and set it off. The bright light lit up the sky for just a second but, Haakon hoped, it would be long enough for the people on the other island to see.

He waited and watched, far into the night, for a return signal. There was none. Haakon could remain on his island forever, trying to get somebody else's attention, but it might never work. The only answer was to go to the other island. And he would begin the preparations first thing in the morning.

When morning came, Haakon removed the vines that had grown over his failed canoe and studied the vessel. The problem was balance. He took up a sheet of canvas and some charcoal and began drawing.

It took two tries before Haakon got it right. He worked frantically every day, and every evening he climbed to his lookout perch and watched the smoke that curled from the fire. Whoever was there was still there, almost as if they were waiting for Haakon. He would not disappoint them.

When the boat was finished, it had a balancing beam out to one side of it, loaded with ballast to keep it from tipping. It also had a sail, made from his hammock, and a rudder, made from the paddle he'd carved. It wasn't as graceful as the *Flora*, but it floated, it moved with the wind, and it would carry him.

It took the better part of a day for Haakon to sail the few miles. Being uncertain what he would find, he was glad for the cover of night when he arrived. He pulled his boat ashore down the island's coast from where he'd seen the fire night after night. He hid it under the cover of palm fronds and approached the fireside by creeping through the undergrowth.

What he saw were people, but people unlike any he'd ever seen before. Haakon knew that they must be natives from one of the nearby islands. He hid and watched.

Then two of them emerged from a hut, pulling somebody with them. Haakon couldn't believe his eyes. He couldn't contain his excitement, either.

"Mary!" he whispered, wanting to yell, but he held back, wondering fearfully just what was going on.

When the native yanked at Mary's arm one more time, he could no longer contain himself. He had to save her.

He bounded out of the undergrowth, pulling out his saber with one hand and his pistol with the other.

Haakon leapt into the clearing, knocking the two young native boys to the sand with a single blow.

Mary screamed.

That brought about twenty other natives immediately. They circled Haakon. He wasn't afraid.

"*Haakon?* I knew you were alive. I knew it!" Mary called. She ran to him to hug him. He brushed her away.

"This is no time for a reunion! I've got to get you out of here!"

There was no way Haakon could fight off more than twenty natives. He recognized that he would have to frighten them off to make time for a getaway. He swept around the circle, brandishing his saber and waving his pistol wildly.

"Wait, Haakon, you don't — "

"I have a boat at the beach. I'll fight them off as long as I can!"

"Haakon," she said insistently.

And then he heard another voice, almost as welcome as Mary's.

"What you going to do, kid, take on the whole village by yourself?"

"Jens!" Haakon said. "Come on, we can take them together!" He tossed a long knife to Jens who began laughing.

"They're friends, Haakon. These guys saved our lives!" Jens said. Then he pointed to Haakon and said something in an unfamiliar language to the natives who relaxed the circle around Haakon.

"They plucked us out of the ocean," Mary explained. "We've been traveling from island to island with them, trying to find you."

"But why were you fighting with them?" Haakon asked, still confused.

"These boys?" Mary said. "We have a slight misunderstanding, see. They claimed me as their sister, and now they think that means I'm supposed to clean up after them. They're wrong."

"She fights with them every night," Jens said.

Suddenly, the humor of the whole situation came to Haakon — how foolish he'd been, how silly the boys were who wanted Mary to clean, how funny she was about refusing it, and how utterly ridiculous Haakon must have looked brandishing pistol and saber to protect somebody like Mary who really didn't need protecting.

Haakon began laughing. Jens and Mary joined in. Soon the natives were laughing as well. Haakon laughed until the tears rolled down his cheeks. He laughed because it was funny, he laughed because it was wonderful. He laughed because he had almost forgotten how wonderful life could be. He laughed because he was with friends.

Chapter 17

There was so much to tell Mary and Jens! Haakon accepted the food the natives cooked for him, and the three friends sat around the fire Haakon had watched so many times from his own island, and they talked.

"Howell's real name's Merrick, and he's a pirate," Haakon explained. "And *I've* got his treasure. A fortune! It's Xanadu, Mary — just like in the book. I could pay for my parent's farm and still have enough left over to buy Norway!"

"I knew something was wrong with him," Jens said. "I should have seen through the disguise."

"You really found a genuine pirate's treasure?" Mary asked.

"Where do you think I got this," Haakon said, showing her and Jens the spyglass, "and these." He took off the ruby necklace and gave it to Mary. "I wanted to give this to you the moment I found it."

Mary held the necklace up to the fire and watched the red of its stones glow in the light of the dancing flames.

"It's beautiful."

"There's lots more where that came from. I'll share it with you both. We'll go back tomorrow."

The three of them agreed to return to the island the next day. They planned to collect the treasure from Haakon's island and then rejoin the natives who would help them find their way to a port with a ship to return home.

The next morning they took off for Haakon Island, as Haakon told them he had named it. The natives loaned them two dugout canoes, and Haakon admired their craftsmanship more than he wanted to admit. He studied them carefully and tried not to compare them to the strange vessel he himself had made. He couldn't help it, though, and when he did, he found that he'd really done all right for a farm boy from Norway.

It took less than two hours to reach Haakon Island. Haakon pointed out the remains of the wreckage of the *Flora* and had them land on the beach nearest the big tree.

"The treasure is in a hiding place in the jungle," he explained. "We have to drag the canoes there to load them up."

They began the journey. Haakon was proud of his island, proud of his home. He enjoyed showing it off to Mary and Jens, telling them stories of how he had taken care of himself during the months he'd been alone.

"That tree has the best bananas," he said. "It's the angle of the sun, I think. And there, that's where I got my first coconut. . . ."

Mary and Jens listened in rapt attention, as interested in hearing the tale as Haakon was in telling it.

Suddenly Haakon's hand went up. "Stop!"

Jens and Mary halted immediately.

"What's the matter?" Mary asked.

"One of my booby traps," Haakon explained. "I put them all over the island."

"For what?" Jens asked.

"If the pirates left treasure here, they'll come back for it someday. But, see, it's my treasure now."

Haakon thought he saw Jens wink at Mary. "A man has to protect what's his," he said.

Then Haakon showed them the first booby trap. "It's over there, by the tree," he said. Jens looked at the ropes and pulleys Haakon had salvaged from the ship. "Step on that vine and you'll be swinging from the top of that tree. Stay close to me, now. I know where they all are."

Jens and Mary stayed close to Haakon.

When evening came, Haakon cooked them a meal of potatoes that he had grown from the ones he'd found on the ship, and fish, fried in palm oil with wild onions that grew on the island.

"I'm impressed, Haakon," Jens said. "You've put together quite a place here."

"It's a real Xanadu, fit for a king," Mary said.

Xanadu. Haakon had longed for it and dreamed of it for all the months he'd been there by himself. And now Mary thought he'd been in Xanadu all the time. He now realized it hadn't been true. Not when he was alone.

"I felt like a king here," Haakon said. "But it wasn't like home."

The word *home* seemed to sweep over all three of them. They shared a homesickness for three different homes that the three of them might never see again. After a few minutes of quiet, Haakon suggested that they rest for the night. "Tomorrow I'll take you to the wreck of the *Flora* and to the cave where I found the treasure."

Jens smiled and lifted his coconut shell filled with fresh cool water. He offered a toast. "To bringing the treasure home!"

Haakon and Mary clinked coconut shells with him.

Chapter 18

"I can't believe you ever got out of there alive the first time!" Jens said, wiping the dust and cobwebs off himself as the trio emerged from the pirates' cave.

"I almost didn't," Haakon admitted. "Listen, we'd better get back and pack up the canoes so we can leave first thing in the morning."

He showed Mary and Jens the shortcut back to the tree. As they rounded the hillside, Mary looked out over the ocean. She gasped.

"A ship! A ship!" she cried.

Haakon and Jens looked, too. She was right. There, a few miles away from the island and headed right in their direction, was a ship.

Mary ran down off the path and onto the beach. Haakon paused, looking between two rocks, wondering if his eyes deceived him. Jans stood by him, shading his eyes with his hand. It was, indeed, a ship. It was a fair-sized one, with three masts and flags flying. Then, at the same moment, Haakon and

Jens identified the topmost flag. It was black, with a white skull and crossbones on it.

It was a pirate ship.

Haakon and Jens ran to stop Mary.

"We're rescued! We're rescued!" she shouted, waving both of her hands and calling at the top of her voice.

Haakon and Jens caught up with her and grabbed her arms.

"What are you doing?"

"They're pirates!" Jens said.

Mary's face paled. A few seconds before, she'd felt that they'd all be saved. Now, she feared, they were looking at their death sentences.

"Let's get off the island, now!" Mary urged.

"It's too late," Jens said. "They're dropping anchor."

Haakon took Mary's wrist. "Come on," he said. "We have to get out of sight."

The three of them returned to the thick underbrush of the island where they could not be spotted.

"We're outnumbered and they have guns," Jens reasoned. "There's no use trying to fight them."

"I agree, but perhaps we can outsmart them," Haakon said. "We can hide out until dark and then sneak off the island. In the meantime, let's make sure the treasure is safely hidden in my tree."

The threesome had a brief period to prepare themselves. They then hid behind some rocks and watched the longboat full of pirates approach Haakon Island. There were three pirates and the captain aboard. As soon as the captain stepped out, Haakon,

Jens, and Mary knew they were in for trouble.

"It's Howell," Jens hissed.

"You mean Merrick," Haakon corrected him. "He's come back for his treasure."

"He's in for a surprise," Mary said.

"I'll say," said Haakon. "He's heading right for one of my traps. That ought to thin them out a little!"

They crouched in their hiding place and watched the troop of pirates approach the trap Haakon had laid with the ship's anchor. Merrick stepped right on the trip vine. Haakon held his breath and waited.

The bowline released perfectly. The rope slipped away from the tree. The anchor was released. It swung in a wide arc and immediately became stuck in the plentiful new growth that the tree had sprouted since Haakon had laid the trap. Merrick and the pirates not only didn't get hurt. They didn't even notice!

"It didn't work!" Mary hissed.

"I didn't count on the tree growing so fast," Haakon said, a little disgusted with himself. "Well, there are plenty more."

Haakon took out the spyglass and watched and waited. Merrick and his men reached the section of the ravine right below the cave. Haakon looked at the booby trap he'd set there. Dozens of boulders were perched above the entrance, waiting to be pulled down onto an unsuspecting pirate who picked the wrong vine to climb.

Without hesitation, Merrick reached for the vine that Haakon had notched, the one and only one that would raise him safely to the cave. He hoisted himself up. His men followed — using the same vine, one by one.

"I can't believe it," Haakon said.

"Don't any of them work?" Mary asked.

"I don't know," Haakon told her.

Merrick emerged from the cave a few seconds later, bellowing angrily.

"I want my treasure found! I want whoever done this dead! No one steals John Merrick's treasure and lives to toast a drink to it!"

Haakon realized with an unpleasant sinking feeling that Merrick was talking about him.

"I want every tree, every rock, every hole in this island searched! Now! Every inch!"

The pirates began planning the search among themselves.

"And if we find whoever done this, we'll bury them up to their noses in the sand and let them watch the tide come in!"

Haakon looked to Mary and Jens for courage. They were afraid, too.

"No!" Merrick continued. "Better yet! We'll bury them up to their neck only. Then we can hear them scream!"

They'd heard enough. The three of them backed away from the beach and the cave. They snuck off, staying close to the rocks for shelter from the pirates' sharp eyes.

Haakon led the way to his tree and took Jens and Mary up to his own personal crow's nest. From there they could see everything that was happening without being seen themselves.

The pirates followed some of the paths that Haakon had cut while living on the island. The trail they were on would lead right through the trap with the pot of rocks and the gunpowder.

Haakon held his breath and crossed his fingers. There was Merrick, aiming right at one of the most deadly traps. With each step, he closed the gap and came closer to the moment of his downfall. . . .

Merrick's foot tripped the vine. Haakon took in a gasp of air. The bowline knot holding the pot slipped, and then stopped. The pot dangled three feet lower than it had been for months, but it didn't move another inch.

Haakon couldn't believe it. He couldn't even look at his friends.

Before he knew it, Merrick and his gang of three had reached the big tree where all the treasure was stowed and camouflaged. Merrick sat down on a log next to the hidden entrance — right below Haakon and his friends.

"Go back to the ship," Merrick commanded. "Get the rest of our men. We'll need help to search the entire island."

"Aye aye, Captain," Jim Thatcher said. Haakon was no happier to see his face than he had been to see Merrick's. He hated to think what Thatcher would bring back with him from the ship.

"And have a couple of them slaves row an extra boat with supplies. We'll be spending the night here. The rest of them I want locked up."

Haakon and Jens looked at one another. If Merrick had "slaves" with him, that could mean allies for them! Maybe, just maybe, they might have a chance.

Mary's foot slipped in the cramped crow's nest, jostling a piece of fruit that they'd brought up with them. It tumbled down from the top of the tree and landed right next to Merrick.

He stood and looked up, curiously examining the source of the fruit. He knew the big old tree wasn't a fruit tree. There could be no explanation except —

"Chp, chp, tsssss!" The bold little monkey who had challenged Haakon by tossing things at him came running along a branch of the big tree, and tossed a coconut at Merrick.

"Cursed apes!" Merrick hissed back angrily at the little creature. He pulled his pistol from his belt and fired a shot. The monkey escaped easily.

Above them, high in the crow's nest, Haakon, Mary, and Jens breathed again.

Merrick walked down the hill to the beach to wait for his reinforcements.

Jens, Haakon, and Mary remained in the crow's nest, knowing it was the one place on the island where they were safe. Merrick was hardly going to look up into the branches of a tree for treasure, and he wasn't likely to stay below it if he thought he'd get hit with another mango.

Chapter 19

"Jens, look!" Haakon said later, pointing to the long-boats that were coming to the island from the ship.

Jens took the spyglass. "Berg and Steine!" he said, identifying the two slaves who were rowing the pirates. They *would* have allies in their fight against Merrick. "Thank goodness they're still alive. And that means our other mates probably are, too."

When night fell, the pirates made camp on the beach. Haakon, Jens, and Mary lowered themselves from the crow's nest and snuck in behind the big fire Merrick's men had built. Berg and Steine sat on a log nearby with their hands and feet bound.

"We're not leaving without them," Haakon whispered to Jens, who agreed.

"Come on. I've got an idea," Jens said.

They returned to the hollow tree where the three of them worked quickly to put the treasure into Hakon's homemade sailboat.

"There are probably only two pirate guards," Jens told Haakon. "If you get past them all right, you release our mates and take over the ship."

Haakon nodded agreement. Mary didn't.

"This is so stupid," she said. "I'm the one who should go. Haakon knows the island best, and you, Jens, know everything else."

Jens and Haakon looked at one another. "She might have a point," Jens said.

"No!" Haakon said.

Mary put her hands on her hips and confronted Haakon. "Why?" she demanded. "Because I'm a girl?"

"Yes," Haakon replied automatically. "It's too dangerous."

She stepped forward and faced him directly. "I snuck on board *your* ship when *you* were standing guard. I'll get past those pirates better than you ever could!"

Haakon was bewildered, but Jens said, "I believe her." Haakon reconsidered the logic and relented.

"All right. But be careful."

Without a word, Mary climbed into the boat and prepared for the short voyage to the ship.

"Wait for our signal, then carry out the plan," Jens said.

"But what if you're captured or . . ." She couldn't bear to finish the thought.

"That's not going to happen," Haakon said as positively as he could. "But if it does, you sail without us. Take my share of the treasure to my family."

Without further ado, Jens and Haakon gave the sailboat a shove and Mary was gone.

* * *

Mary had been raised near the sea. She knew how to sail, **ev**en by moonlight and even with an overladen, cumbersome sailboat. She maneuvered the craft to the far side of the pirate ship and drew close to the windows of the captain's cabin at the ship's stern. It was one place she was sure would be empty tonight.

She'd seen two men on the deck, undoubtedly the watchmen the captain had left. Her job was to get inside the ship and release the slaves who could then overpower the two men on watch.

She fastened the little sailboat to the rear of the ship and prepared to climb in through one of the open windows of Merrick's cabin. She took hold of the windowsill and pulled herself up, but as she did so, one of her feet kicked the little paddle she'd used as a rudder and it splashed into the sea.

Mary could hear the thumping of the pirates' feet as they ran to the edge of the ship to see what had made the noise. Mary was safely inside the cabin but when she looked out, she could see the sailboat beneath her. The pirates would surely see it, too.

Then, as if on cue, a gentle breeze pushed the homemade boat around to the far side of the ship, completely out of view of the watchmen.

"Probably just a fish jumped," Mary heard one voice say above her.

"Let's drink to 'em!" the other suggested.

Mary breathed a sigh of relief.

Chapter 20

The sun rose on Haakon Island. The pirates and their captain were waking up slowly. One rubbed his eyes, another stretched. The fire from the night before still smoldered. There was a thin stream of smoke rising from the few remaining red coals.

Haakon and Jens circled the camp to get as close as possible, yet remain hidden. And then the moment came.

Haakon tossed an entire box filled with rockets salvaged from the *Flora* into the remains of the pirates' camp fire.

The explosions were deafening. At once, all of the pirates jumped up, wide awake.

"We're under attack! Spread out!" Merrick screamed. The pirates fled in chaos.

In an instant the beach was deserted, except for Berg, Steine, and the one pirate assigned to watch them. He would not dare leave his post, even under attack.

He glanced around fearfully. Then he saw someone in a white shirt running swiftly through the forest.

"Over here! They're over here!" he shouted to his mates, and he could no longer contain himself. He fled after the culprit. He didn't have time to notice that the "culprit" he chased was actually a little monkey wearing a Norwegian ship's boy's shirt. The pirate was knocked cold by Jens before he had time to see anything at all.

Jens turned to his mates, Merrick's captives.

"Some party, huh, mates?" he asked.

"Jens!" Berg said, stunned, but glad to be freed by Jens' sharp knife.

"And Haakon," Steine said. "We thought you two were dead for sure!"

"And we will be if we don't get out of here!" Jens said. Without another word, the four men fled from the beach, away from the hunting pirates.

"Where are we running to?" Berg asked.

"To canoes and then to the ship. With any luck, Mary's on board and has released our mates."

"What if she wasn't lucky?" Steine asked.

Haakon didn't answer. It wasn't anything he really wanted to think about. After all, they'd come so far. Could they fail now?

"Over there!" a pirate shouted across a ravine, spotting Haakon and his mates.

"Come on, we're taking a shortcut!" Haakon said.

Jens, Berg, and Steine followed him, although the trail was through much rougher terrain. They tumbled along the trail, stumbling and rolling where the mountain led down to the sea.

However, it turned out they weren't the only ones who had spotted the shortcut, for there were pirates above them and pirates ahead, below them.

"We're boxed in!" Haakon said.

"Wait here!" Jens said. "I'm going to have some fun. When the coast is clear, take off again. I'll catch up."

Jens didn't pause for any further explanation; he was off like a shot from a pistol. Haakon showed Berg and Steine where they could duck behind a boulder for some cover. It would hide them for a few minutes at least.

Jens led the pirates on a wild chase. He was fast and agile from years of climbing on ship's rigging. Soon, he had all four pirates on his tail.

"Hey! Over here!" he yelled. They aimed and fired. Jens disappeared, flying into the dense jungle.

When the pirates were out of sight after him, Haakon began the descent with Berg and Steine. He drew them to a halt at the edge of a steep ravine.

"Some shortcut, Haakon," Berg complained. "Now we're trapped! And what about Jens?"

"This is my island, Berg. No one traps me on it," Haakon told him.

Then he brought out the dagger he'd taken from the pirate treasure, reached for a vine, and cut it with a single slice. The ship's wheel from the *Flora* tumbled down out of a mass of vines above. Some vines were tied to it as well. It was a gigantic swing.

"Grab hold of it," Haakon instructed them. "You two swing over first. I'm waiting for Jens."

Steine looked at the deep gorge in front of him. "You've gone crazy, lad," he said.

There was gunfire behind them. The pirates were firing at Jens! Then, on the hill to their right, Jens was in the open, running for his life.

The pirates were gaining. Jens stumbled, giving them another few precious seconds to catch up with him. Jens righted himself and began running as fast as he could.

Suddenly everything changed. Jens tripped one of Haakon's booby traps. Four trees, tied to the ground by vines, were released, springing upward, held together by an expanse of sail that carried Jens up, up, and away!

"What was that?" Steine cried out.

"A mistake," Haakon began and then, watching Jens soar through the air toward some more vines, thought that it might just have saved Jens' life! Nimbly, as Haakon had seen him do a hundred times on the *Flora*, Jens grabbed a vine to break his fall, swung through on it, and lowered himself to the ground, safely out of reach of the pursuing pirates. He began running once again.

Haakon returned his attention to Steine and Berg. This was no time for watching. It was time for action. "Swing over now, or I'll push you," Haakon said, finally convincing them to cross the ravine. Once they were safely over, they swung the ship's wheel back, and Haakon grabbed it.

He had to wait for his friend.

"Jens!" Haakon cried.

He was answered by someone else.

"And it's you who got my treasure!" Merrick growled. He was standing about five feet above Haakon on the hill. Merrick had a saber in one hand and a pistol in the other. Haakon thought he was done for until he realized that Merrick was also about a half a foot from one of Haakon's own booby traps. Haakon stood speechless as his mind raced.

"You needn't worry about your tongue no more, young Haakon. It's your whole head I'll be hanging from the halyard. *After* you show me to my treasure!"

Jens emerged from the jungle and stopped dead next to Haakon before he realized that Haakon had been caught. Breathing hard, he remained silent.

Haakon spoke. "Aye aye, sir," he said. Then slowly, deliberately, Haakon stepped backward down the hill, first one step and then another. He put his hand across Jens' chest and brought him along. He just had to lure Merrick into the trap, but he had to be careful, too. One false step for them and Merrick would put bullets in them. Then it wouldn't matter what happened to the booby trap Haakon had laid.

Merrick was suspicious. "Don't be fooling with me, boy!" he threatened, brandishing the pistol at the two of them. "I mean it, boy!"

Haakon crossed his fingers for luck and inched back.

Merrick took the bait. He stepped forward, and tripped the trap. Before Merrick knew what had happened to him, he was hanging upside down from a vine suspended from a palm tree. He was utterly astonished, but not too astonished to try firing his gun. He did so, but he was swinging so wildly that the bullet didn't get anywhere near its target. Haakon didn't think he and Jens should take a chance that they would be that lucky again.

"Let's go!" They swung across the ravine, dropped down onto the beach, and ran for the canoes. Haakon grabbed a paddle and ran the boat into the water, quickly catching up with Berg and Steine. He was only vaguely aware of the fury of Merrick, shouting at his pirates.

"Up here, you idiots! *Here! Here!!!* They're going to the ship! After them! After them!!"

Merrick didn't even want his men to cut him loose. That could wait. He knew now that the only chance of victory would be for the longboat to catch up to the canoes.

Although the canoes had a head start, the longboat had the advantage of speed. Jim Thatcher stood in the front of the longboat as it bounded across the sea, closing the gap between it and the canoes.

Haakon was fairly sure that the motion of the boat would make it impossible for Thatcher to shoot with any accuracy as long as they were still in pursuit, but the minute the longboat caught up with the canoes —

"Booooom!" The sound of a cannon burst through Haakon's thoughts. There was a loud splash as a cannonball landed in the water right by the longboat.

"Mary!" Haakon cried. Now there was hope!

She stood on the side of the ship, surrounded by Haakon's mates from the *Flora*, waving encouragingly. Then, on her signal, another cannonball flew loudly through the air, this time so close to the longboat that its wake turned the boat over, dumping the pirates into the sea.

"Hoist the mainsails!" Mary cried.

"Aye aye, ma'am," the bosun responded. Haakon watched the sails fly up the masts.

Thatcher and his crew of three sputtered in the water, trying to reach their overturned boat, but before they could do it, Mary gave one more signal. This cannonball landed squarely on the overturned longboat, splintering it and erasing all hope the pirates might have had of catching up with the canoes.

The pirates then swam, wildly trying to reach the ship before it could sail. They didn't want to be left alone on a small island with their angry, foul-tempered captain.

All Haakon could see was Mary. She stood on the deck, gave orders, and cheered him on. Her eyes flashed with excitement at their victory. She was in command of the ship.

Then his canoe bumped into the ship. Haakon reached blindly, grabbing onto the rope ladder his mates tossed down to him and to Jens. Berg and Steine scrambled up it as well, pulling the ladder up behind them in case any of the pirates should have an idea about boarding the ship.

Mary gave the command for a final salute with the cannon. The ball shot out across the narrow stretch of water that separated them from the island — and Merrick's treachery — and landed on the beach right beneath Merrick's upended nose, scattering sand all over the pirate. Haakon and his shipmates laughed with joy at the sight.

Jens mounted the rigging on the mainmast and didn't stop until he got to the very top where the Jolly Roger flew. He took out his knife, cut the lines, and tossed the despised flag into the waters below.

The last sail rose in place. They weighed anchor. Majestically, the ship turned, the sails filling with the warm tropical wind, and headed for home.

Chapter 21

When the snow melted, so it seemed, did all hope. Sarah and Rakel sat at the kitchen table in their farmhouse, watching their mother pack their meager belongings.

"Where are we going to live, Mama?" Sarah asked.

"We have relatives. We can stay with them. For a while. Then, well, things will be fine. Don't you worry."

Mrs. Haakonsen wished she could take her own advice. Life had been so hard for all the years her husband had been at sea. Now with her son gone, she felt helpless and hopeless. She picked up a wooden hammer Haakon had played with as a child. She tried not to let her girls see her tears as she packed it. After all, it was theirs. Wernes hadn't been able to take *everything* from them.

Outside, Mr. Haakonsen began the laborious job of boarding up the windows. That would protect the house in case, just in case, they might one day return to it. His hammer struck rhythmically. He thought of the hammer Mama had packed, the one he'd made for Haakon when he was a lad. His own hammer seemed to say his son's name as he banged on the nails.

Haa-*kon*! Haa-*kon*!

And then the sound changed. It became Pa-*pa*! Pa-*pa*!

The third time, Papa wasn't so sure it was the hammer that was calling his name. The fourth time, he knew it was not. He stopped hammering altogether and turned to face the call. It was faint, but it was there. Then, as if in a dream, Haakon rounded the hill on the road that led to his farmhouse.

"Papa!" he cried, dropping his bag and running from the two friends who had come with him.

Papa put down his hammer and ran to greet his son. Soon his sisters appeared at the door of the farmhouse and ran to Haakon as well.

Haakon held them all in his arms, hugging them as he had never hugged anybody before, treasuring the look of their faces, the joy, the tears of the moment. Not a word was spoken. Everything was said with their embraces.

Then it was time to see his mother. Haakon entered the farmhouse kitchen on tiptoe.

"Mama," he whispered.

She turned around. She stared and gasped, still holding the little wooden hammer in her hand.

"Mama," he said, louder this time. "It's me, Haakon."

Tears welled up in the woman's tired face. She began laughing at the same time, opening her arms for him.

"I missed you, Mama. I missed you so!"

"Haakon," was all she said. It was all she could say.

The next few minutes were a jumble of hugs and introductions. Mama, Papa, Rakel, and Sarah hugged Jens and Mary as well. Then, when everybody had hugged and been hugged, Haakon noticed all the boxes in the house.

"Why are you packing?" Haakon asked.

The joyous mood dissipated. "We lost the farm, Haakon. Wernes let us stay through winter but now we have to go."

A big smile crossed Haakon's face. "No, we don't," Haakon said. Then he reached into his pocket and pulled out some papers. "See, I bought it this morning!"

Chapter 22

Six weeks later, the Haakonsen farm looked like new. The crops were planted, and already there were signs of green sprouts in the fields. The house had been repaired and painted. Everything was shipshape and in running order.

Haakon had a surprise for Mary. He'd come from the village post office and run all the way home, clutching the gift in his hand. He waved to his father and Jens, working in the new shed next to the farm, and ran straight to the tall birch tree behind the farm. He mounted the branches quickly and settled down at the top where he and Jens had fashioned a crow's nest. Mary was looking at the countryside from her perch there.

"It's for me?" she said, looking curiously at the package.

"I sent all the way to London for it," he told her and then watched excitedly as she opened it.

It was a small, brown leather-bound book of verse. The pages were gold on the edges and the endpapers were swirls of bright colors.

"It's to replace the one that was ruined," he said.

Mary smiled. "That was nice, Haakon. I love it," she said, opening the book and looking at the pages. "Am I home now?" she asked. "Am I really home?"

Haakon nodded. "For as long as you want," he said.

Then, below them, there was an indignant shriek.

"Help!" a muffled voice yowled.

"What was that?" Mary asked.

Haakon shrugged modestly. "Just one of the booby traps I set up to protect the farm from intruders," he said.

They peered over the edge of the crow's nest. There, strung up by his feet, was none other than Ole, the bully.

"He's such a baby," Haakon said. "He's afraid of his own shadow, you know."

Jens laughed first. Then Papa and Haakon and Mary were laughing as well.

Haakon thought it was wonderful to be able to laugh, but it was best to be able to laugh with friends and family — in Xanadu.